ADIRONDACK GOLD

FIC
GRA
c.1

ADIRONDACK GOLD

Persis Granger

Drawings and cover design by Laurel A. Granger

Beaver Meadow Publishing
Thurman, NY

Adirondack Gold

All Rights Reserved © 2003 by Persis Granger

No part of this book may be reproduced or transmitted in any form or by any means, graphic, electronic, or mechanical, including photocopying, recording, taping, or by any information storage retrieval system, without written permission from the publisher. Reviewers may quote brief passages to be printed in a magazine or newspaper.

Beaver Meadow Publishing
Persis Granger
Town of Thurman
11 Clarence Russell Road
Warrensburg, NY 12885
www.persisgranger.com

ISBN: 0-9742085-0-7
Library of Congress Control Number: 2003093970

Printed in the United States of America
Second Printing in November 2003
Patterson Printing
1550 Territorial Road
Benton Harbor, MI 49022

Edited by Robin Granger
Designed by Stephen Buckbee

To the people of the Town of Thurman

and

To those who discover and collect, preserve and
protect its history.

Contents

Illustrations

Drawings

Maps

Maps were drawn by Richard D. Granger.

Preface

Adirondack Gold is a made-up tale about make-believe characters—fiction, in other words—set in the real-life town of Thurman, NY, about 1895.

Thurman was named for its founder, John Thurman, who held title to a large tract of land in the southern Adirondack Mountains in the late 1700s. In 1792 the New York State legislature officially created from his holdings the Town of Thurman, a large town of about 800 square miles. This new town encompassed most of Warren County, NY, except for the towns of Queensbury and Lake Luzerne. As the population of Thurman grew, due in large part to the marketing and business efforts of its founder, various sections of it broke away and were established as separate towns, beginning in 1798. By the time our story begins, seven other towns had been formed, and the Town of Thurman was left with 97 square miles. It is bounded on the south by Stony Creek, the east by Warrensburg and Chester, the west by Wells, and the north by Johnsburg, where Crane Mountain stands.

Over the years Thurman was a community of small family farms, with lots of logging and some mining, as well. Almost every stream of any size supported one or more sawmills and gristmills. The bustling town was home to many stores, hotels and boarding houses. Tourists flocked to the region by train and stagecoach to hunt, fish, hike and enjoy the fresh mountain air and hearty country food.

Barbara McMartin tells us in her book *Hides, Hemlocks and Adirondack History* (North Country Books, 1992) that during the mid- to late-1800s, many people earned money by harvesting the bark of hemlock trees and hauling it to the tanneries that operated in nearly every town around Thurman. With sleighs or wagons drawn by horses or oxen, they drove huge loads of the bark as much as ten miles to the tannery yards. There the bark was piled high to be ground up in the bark-grinding sheds, where fires were a constant threat. The tannery workers would layer hides and ground bark in large vats, and then add water. The hides had to soak in this solution for months before they could be used to make shoes, boots and gloves. Toward the end of the 1800s it became too difficult to find near these tanneries enough hemlock bark to keep them supplied, and one by one, the tanneries—those that hadn't already burned—closed their doors. By 1895, when our story takes place, the Adirondack tannery era had ended, but memories lingered on.

As years went by, times changed. It became increasingly difficult to support a family on a small Thurman farm, so more and more residents needed to find paying jobs outside the town. Modern transportation made it possible to drive to larger towns to find not only work, but stores and recreation, as well. Fewer businesses remained open. Thurman became primarily a residential community.

My husband, two daughters and I moved to an old farm in Thurman in 1976, planning to restore the house and outbuildings and grow all our own food. As we peeled a century of wallpaper from the farmhouse walls, we found names inscribed in ornate script on the grainy plaster. When we padded in sock feet up the stairs hollowed by generations of feet before ours, we had an overwhelming sense of time gone by and voices gone silent. History reached out and grabbed us.

Dusty canning jars found in the attic and cobweb-draped hand tools that hung in the barn told the story of a time when hard work and sweat had wrung from this farm a livelihood for its people. Standing in the barn loft, we could conjure up the smell of fresh-cut timothy and clover, the banter of men forking hay up to the barn rafters while a team of draft horses waited patiently to return to fetch the next wagonload from the field.

During the 1970s and '80s we worked to reclaim the fallow fields and failing buildings, and raised all our own chicken, pork, beef, eggs and vegetables. We foraged for wild apples, berries and fiddleheads, and laid in a supply of wood that was our primary source of heat. It was hard work, and at the end of a busy day, as I rested chore-weary bones beside the tan enameled kitchen wood stove, I would think how difficult it must have been to accomplish these tasks and raise a family without electricity—and the accompanying stove, refrigerator, freezer, washing machine and dryer. And what about getting in all that firewood without a chainsaw to cut it and a tractor to haul it? On subzero winter nights, as I heard the furnace click on to supplement the heat of the woodstoves, I wondered, What would life be like without the backup heat of an oil furnace? What must life have been like in Thurman in the 1800s?

Trying to imagine life in so-called "simpler" times prompted the writing of this book. Before I could write, however, I had much to learn. That's when I became acquainted with the *The Quarterly*, a publication of the John Thurman Historical Society. Neil Campbell eagerly shared with me editions published in the '60s and '70s, and supplemented the stories written there with his own recollections of Thurman in the 1920s, '30s and '40s. I quickly learned that, since electricity and telephone had been slow to establish a toe-hold in Thurman, many of our senior citizens remembered from their childhoods a lifestyle very similar to that of their nineteenth century forefathers. I didn't have to guess what life without modern conveniences was like; I had only to ask, so ask I did.

I learned many other things by observing the larger Thurman community as well, for traditional small town events were going on all around me. Rex and Jean Reynolds hosted the town's annual jack wax party for charity every spring. Mae Rozell, with Gloria and Myra Magee, organized town Christmas parties modeled after those held years ago in the old one-room schoolhouses here. The Thurman Volunteer Fire Department raised funds by holding a Fiddlers' Roundup. The Thurman Baptists added a wing onto their church with donated materials and work bees. Over the years the community came together countless times to help a neighbor in time of trouble by holding an auction or a spaghetti supper at the town hall, or organizing a door-to-door collection. It was all one big history lesson, for Thurman is a community whose traditional values have been preserved and nurtured.

Adirondack Gold is intended to be a reflection of these Thurman values and the kind of people who preserve them. It is also intended to depict accurately what the north end of Thurman would have been like around 1895, with its Baptist Church, general store and District Three Schoolhouse all serving as focal points for the community.

Throughout the book I have been careful not to deviate from the facts as I know them, with just one glaring exception. In the story we are told that the name "Centerbar" was derived from the French name "St. Hubert." My research yielded evidence that the name is actually a corruption of "St. Aubin," but I chose to exercise artistic license on this particular point. Other surnames and Christian names in the story were chosen because they are names that have been in common usage in Thurman in the last two centuries. No character in the story is intended to represent any real person, living or dead. They were created solely from my imagination and never lived in Thurman or anywhere else.

I hope that now, however, they will find a home in the hearts of the readers of *Adirondack Gold*.

Acknowledgements

This work is made possible, in part, by public funds from the New York State Council on the Arts Decentralization Program, administered locally by the Lower Adirondack Regional Arts Council. I am most grateful to the LARAC Board of Directors for their support of this undertaking.

State of the Arts

NYSCA

I wish to acknowledge, also, the help of Thurman Town Historian, Robin Croissant, who has worked so passionately to preserve information about Thurman's past, and who has always been willing to share gems of information from her files.

Paula Barclay and Astrid Elliott have generously imparted knowledge about youngsters and reading, gleaned from their many years of elementary school teaching. They were most helpful to me in the preparation of the *Adirondack Gold Teacher's Guide*.

I found much useful background information about sugaring in *The Maple Sugar Book* by Helen and Scott Nearing (Schocken Books, 1973). Many thanks to those who helped fill in the remaining gaps in my understanding—Mike Hill of Valley Road Maple Farm, in Thurman, Gary Gaudette of Leader Evaporators in St. Albans, VT, and, from the American Maple Museum in Croghan, NY, Leslie and Vera Lyndaker and Hugh Worden.

I thank the members of the John Thurman Historical Society, both those who had the vision required to found the organization in the early 1960s and those who proudly carry the torch today. I cannot adequately express my special appreciation to those members who have endured my endless questions and tapped their memories to respond. From Neil Campbell, Mae Rozell, Delila Walter, Irene

Hall, Jean Reynolds, Doris Bunker, Leila Wood, and Evelyn Russell I gleaned much badly-needed information. I also was captivated and inspired by the magic of their story-telling and their gift of still being able to see past events through the eyes of childhood.

My appreciation to Tom Kennedy for guiding me through the dark and mysterious territory of Web page creation and maintenance.

Merci to Marie Jordan for her gracious help with the French dialogue and the history of St. Hubert.

Special thanks go to my family—Dick, Robin, Laurel, Clark, John and Steve—for exercising patience and sharing skills throughout this endeavor.

Without the help of all of these folks, I could not have completed *Adirondack Gold*.

1

Trouble in Warrensburg

By the time Hollis Ingraham left the schoolyard he was moving at a dead run. He knew it would be dark by the time he got home. He hadn't meant to stay so late, but now the golden autumn sun had dipped behind the rim of the Adirondack Mountains. The blazing archway of the sugar maples that lined his path became a darkening tunnel. The houses along his route faded into the evening, then sprang back to life one by one, as lanterns were lit and placed in the windows to welcome their families home. Hollis felt that he could see into those homes. In his mind he saw the mothers, the fathers, the children, dinners on the tables. In his heart he could hear the laughter, feel the love. He ached with longing and ran faster.

This evening of late September bit through his too-small, threadbare coat. He tried to pull it around his body, but it insisted on flapping out behind him like wings, as though willing him to fly. His lungs were on fire, but still he couldn't slow down. There was the abandoned tannery, its ghostly smokestacks and bark piles eerily outlined against the night sky. "Burhans, Gray & Co.," it said on the side of the building. Even though it was too dark to actually read it, he recited it anyway, like a ritual. He always did when he passed. "Burhans, Gray & Co." As always, he pronounced it "coe"

1

rather than "company" as it was intended. And as always, he shuddered and looked away, hastening his pace even more. There was a stench of death at the tannery, and it chased him.

Down the hill, across the bridge, feet pounding, heart pounding, lungs screaming. Hollis didn't slow his pace until he reached the postage-stamp yard in front of the shabby River Street cottage that was home to him and his mother. It was utterly dark. Ma wasn't home yet. Panting, he passed through the gap in the rickety fence where the gate had long ago rotted off its hinges. He slipped down the narrow alley between his house and its neighboring twin. Climbing the back steps and skipping the broken one, he hesitated a moment on the back stoop. Then he made himself enter the pitch-black kitchen.

His practiced hand reached for the iron matchbox that hung on the wall behind the cold enamel stove. He took one of the few remaining matches there and struck it briskly on the raspy plaster of the wall. It sprang to life, and that small circle of brightness led him to the kerosene lantern centered on the tidy square of oilcloth on the rickety kitchen table. In a moment he had the lantern glowing and he shook out the match, satisfied that at least Ma wouldn't have to come home to a dark house. He knew she'd been out making the rounds, asking for work. Every day since the woolen mill shut down, she had gone up Elm Street and down Main Street, stopping at each house, shop and hotel, sometimes finding someone who needed her to do some household chores for a small wage. It was never enough.

Hollis shivered. The unheated house seemed colder than the outdoors. Ma would be chilled when she got here. He picked up the coal hod, remembering only then that there was no more coal, no more money to buy it and no more credit to beg it. Grabbing the lamp, he stepped back out into the yard, surveying the area for something that would burn. He loaded the hod with bounty fallen from the giant old maple behind the house. Then, in a decisive moment, he grabbed the spongy board that had rotted off the steps. There! It might as well serve some purpose.

Hollis opened the firebox of the stove and carefully arranged his finds from smallest to largest. He opened the stove's damper, lit the second match and held it under the leaves. Gently blowing, he coaxed the glowing leaves into flame, then the twigs. At last the larger sticks caught, and Hollis broke up the rotten board and added

Heat for a Little While

a few pieces to the fire. He knew there would be heat for a little while, at least until he could crawl under the covers of his bed.

The wood was nearly used up when Ma finally came in, but the kitchen was almost warm. Usually Hollis could tell how her day had gone by reading her face. Tonight her features were a mask, and she kept her eyes lowered.

"How did it go?" he asked finally.

Ma fidgeted with the corner of her apron.

"Did you find any work?"

Ma cleared her throat and busied herself taking a pan of john-nycake out of the cupboard.

"Ma?"

"Yes," she said slowly.

"That's great!" Hollis exclaimed excitedly. "Where?"

Ma didn't answer. When she did speak, it wasn't really an answer, it was one of those maddening things that grownups say when they don't want to tell you something bad. "Hollis, you're getting to be such a young man."

"What does that have to do with it?" he asked, alarm causing his voice to rise.

"I have to talk to you."

Hollis waited anxiously while she chose the exact words she needed.

"You know that things have been difficult lately."

He nodded. Since the mill laid her off her eyes had had worry wrinkles around them all the time. She had even allowed the church ladies to give them some food and clothing.

"It's got so I can't hold my head up when I walk down the street. As hard as I try, the store bill just keeps going up and up. It's a wonder they even give us credit anymore. And the rent is three months past due. It's a good thing the landlord was a friend of your father or we would have been turned out on the street long ago."

Hollis knew all that. Why was Ma going over all this again? Why was she babbling on and on?

"As it is, Mr. Watson says we have be out of the house by the end of the month." Her voice cracked as she finished and she struggled to regain her composure.

Embarrassed, Hollis poured words into the silence. "But you said you've found work now, right? So we can stay, right?"

Ma couldn't meet his gaze. "This is the hardest part," she said, staring at her shoes. She grasped both of his hands in hers, wanting to force him to understand. "I should have prepared you for this, but I just couldn't bring myself to tell you before now." She took a deep breath then and looked him straight in the eye. "We have to be separated for awhile. I've got work at the hotel. I'm going to live in the maid's room in the attic there. Mrs. Emerson will let me have free room and board as part of my pay for doing cooking, cleaning and ironing at the hotel. Without rent to pay, I can put most of my pay toward our bills. And you—"

"I can help!" Hollis exclaimed. "I can quit school and get a job."

"I won't let you quit school," Ma said firmly.

"You never let me help. You always want to keep me tied up in your apron strings!"

"You need your education."

"But, Ma—"

"No 'buts', Hollis. I simply can't afford to keep you with me. I've sent a letter to your father's people, and word came just yesterday that they will keep you till I get on my feet again. You're to go to Thurman and live with your Grandma and Grandpa Ingraham. You'll be picked up tomorrow morning, early," Ma said, scarcely able to control her voice.

"Tomorrow!" Hollis gasped in dismay. "You can't just send me off to live with strangers!"

"Strangers! They're not strangers; they're your grandparents! Hollis, please understand. I've made the best decision I could. I've got to make things right. The best way you can help me now is to go live with them in Thurman, work hard in school and be a good boy." Ma rumpled his hair. She pulled the crisp white tea towel off the johnnycake and cut him a large piece. "Here," she said, handing it to him as thought that would make everything better, "eat this. I'm sorry. There's nothing else. No butter, even." She stretched out her hands in a helpless gesture.

Nothing else. He knew it was true. Nothing else to eat, nothing else to do. He wanted to scream. Ashamed of his emotions, he bolted from the kitchen to bury himself under the coverlet on his bed, pulling the pillow over his head. He pounded his lumpy mattress with both fists, hot tears of rage and frustration streaming down his face, and silent sobs wracking his body. He couldn't let Ma hear him.

If only his father were here. It seemed foolish to think of that. He hardly remembered his father. There was just a faint recollection of golden sunlight and warm laughter, of strong hands lifting him high in the air, of the rich smell of pine sawdust. He should be here. The unfairness of it all released another flood of silent tears, tears that floated Hollis into a troubled, dream-torn sleep.

In his dream he was back at the tannery, only it wasn't Burhans,

Gray & Co. It was another tannery, one he had never seen, only heard about. There was something awful here, and he felt deep dread. He wanted to run away, but a terrible force pulled him in, drawing him down between the seemingly endless rows of bark piles toward the one place he most didn't want to go, to the bark-grinding shed. Now he heard a voice calling to him. "Hollis!" The voice drew him forward.

In his dream he heard the voice again. "Hollis, help me!" It was his father's voice. He knew that, even though he couldn't remember his father's voice. He must go to him, but his feet were leaden. He saw a hand—his father's hand—outstretched toward him, reaching from the shadows of the shed. "Hollis!"

Hollis tried to reach out to the hand, but his arms wouldn't move. He saw then that they were bound to his sides mummy-fashion, wrapped snugly with long white starched apron ties. Frantically he inched his way closer to the hand until he could wrap his fingers around it. Grasping the hand as hard as he could, he began to pull. With horror he felt it squish and crumble in his grip as he wrenched it from the sleeve in the blackness of the shed. He couldn't breathe.

"Hollis!" This time it was Ma's voice.

"Ma! Help!" he gasped.

"Hollis, wake up!" It was his mother again, and his mother's strong hand was gently shaking his shoulder. He opened his eyes and saw her beside him, her face illuminated in the glow of the kerosene lamp. Relief washed over him.

"Ma?" he said.

"It's time to get up, sleepyhead," she said with forced cheerfulness. Then she asked in surprise, "Why, what have you got in your hand?"

With a start Hollis looked down at his clenched fist. Crumbly yellow mush was oozing from it.

"Is that what you did with the johnnycake I gave you last night?" Ma laughed.

Still drowsily unconvinced that it was really cornbread and not the rotting hand of his father, he blinked his eyes, trying to sift dream from reality.

"Never mind that now," Ma said. "You have to get ready to leave."

Leave! A thousand words welled up in his throat. He wanted to beg her to let him stay. He wanted to tell her he wouldn't be any trouble, that he would stay in school, sleep on the floor of her little attic room, do anything, if he just wouldn't have to go away. Instead he buried the feelings deep inside himself and just watched her as she quickly packed the few things he owned into a small cloth flour sack. "Come on," she said with a note of urgency in her voice, "grab your hat and boots and let's get down to the kitchen so we won't keep them waiting."

Down in the kitchen Hollis sat by the window, watching for the wagon that was to pick him up and take him away from everything that he knew and loved. The dark streets of the small Adirondack town were already alive with heavy wagons rumbling toward the markets with loads of produce, hay, and firewood.

Ma was carving off another hunk of johnnycake and packing it in Hollis' dinner pail. "This will help tide you over until you get to your grandma's good cooking." She smiled at him gently. "You remember your grandma, don't you?"

He nodded, struggling to conjure up a picture of her—a somber, dark-haired, black-dressed woman riding stiffly on a farm wagon. He remembered how she touched his cheek with a surprisingly gentle hand that smelled of lye soap and smiled at him with bright blue eyes.

Ma continued, "Of course, they haven't been to see us in years—only once since your father...." Her voice trailed off. She never said it. Never said, "died." It was as though by not saying it, all the pain and loss had never happened. Hollis never said it either.

"Why not?" he asked. "Why didn't they come?"

Ma hesitated. "They thought...they blamed...oh, I don't know. It was all so long ago. They said—well, things were said, and it seemed like there was no turning back."

Just then Hollis spotted a pair of lanterns approaching the house and slowing to a halt. He could barely make out the form of the large wagon from which they hung.

"Ma, they're here!" he exclaimed, fear cracking his voice.

"Come quickly, son," Ma said anxiously, grabbing his hand,

snatching up the sack and dinner pail and heading out the kitchen door.

2

Off to Thurman

Ma stopped abruptly when she reached the side of the wagon. "Why, Gibby Goodnow!" she exclaimed with obvious pleasure. "I thought Father Ingraham would be coming for Hollis!"

The big bear of a man on the wagon snatched the floppy felt hat off his head, his red-bearded round face wreathed with smiles. "Mary! Good to see you! Old Sanford, he woulda come himself, but his bad leg pains him something awful when he sets up on the wagon a long time. So, since I was coming into Warrensburg with a load of firewood yesterday and spending the night at my cousin's, I told him and the missus to let me fetch the boy home." He paused. "My, Mary, but you're a sight for sore eyes!"

"It's good to see you again, too, Gibby."

He turned to Hollis. "So this is my young passenger!" he said then, his warmth dispelling some of the boy's fear. "Haven't seen you since you were a little bit of a thing. Hop up here. We'd best not waste any time."

Gibby raised the reins as if to start up his yoke of oxen, and then hesitated. Gentle concern pushed the joviality from his voice as he looked at Hollis' ma. "Mary, why didn't you tell anyone where you were until now?"

"I just needed to be some place else, to get away."

9

"Away from family and friends?" Gibby asked, as if the idea amazed him.

"It wasn't that simple; you see, they believed that I was responsible for—" Again she stopped. "But that's not what's important now," she said, stowing Hollis' things behind the wagon seat. She pinched back sudden tears. "Just take good care of my boy."

"You know you're doing the best thing," Gibby reassured her, snapping the reins over the oxen.

"Hollis, be good!" Ma called out, walking beside the wagon as they moved out. She reached up to give Hollis' arm one more squeeze. "Write to me!"

Hollis' heart sank as they pulled away from her, and he tried to smile bravely, twisting halfway around on the wagon seat to wave at her until she was out of sight. The wagon bumped along the rutted tracks that ran beside the Schroon River, shrouded in mist this brisk autumn morning. Many times he and his school chums had raced down this very road, chasing after the stagecoach as it made its run to Thurman Station. It was always exciting to see the rail passengers arriving. There would be tourists all decked out in finery few locals could afford; there was the occasional visiting dignitary, or colorful drummer with a valise full of wares. Once there was even a troupe of actors who had come to perform up at the hotel.

As if reading his mind, the gentle giant beside him said affably, "Guess you've been out this way more'n once, eh?"

Hollis nodded. "I like to go out to the station to see the trains. My grandparents don't live near the station, do they?"

Surprise registered on Gibby's face. "Lord, no, boy! Don't you remember where they live?" His face sobered as he answered his own question. "No, I guess you wouldn't. You don't hardly even know your Pa's people, do you? They're good folks, but when your Pa died, it hurt them something awful. Your grandpa—well, it was like something inside him died."

Hollis looked at him in surprise. At last there was someone who would say the word! He ventured a question. "Did you know him— my Pa, I mean?"

"Did I know him!" Fondness was evident in Gibby's broad grin.

"Why me and Johnny Ingraham was like two peas in a pod. We went to school together, we sugared together, we went hunting and fishing together," he paused and winked at Hollis, "and we raised considerable mischief together." Gibby thought for a minute, then added, "We was together the very night he met your ma."

"Really?" Hollis asked. "Where?"

"Over to Mill Creek," Gibby said, pronouncing it "crick." "We was seventeen, eighteen then, and always looking for a good time. We'd heard there was to be a dance over to Mill Creek, so after supper we scrubbed up, slicked back our hair, put on fresh boiled shirts and commenced to walking the seven miles to Mill Creek."

"You walked seven miles just to go to a dance?" Hollis asked incredulously.

Gibby laughed and shook his head. "Son, in those days we woulda walked twenty if dancing and pretty girls was waiting at the other end. There was pretty girls that night, and Mary Reynolds—your ma—was the prettiest of all. We had our photograph taken, the three of us together. Your ma had eyes only for your Pa from that day on."

Hollis pondered on this for awhile, struggling to imagine his mother as a pretty young girl shyly waiting to be asked to dance. Could this be the same Ma that he knew, the woman who dragged herself home exhausted each evening, worry lines etched in her face and weariness carved into her posture?

Gibby interrupted his musings. "But to get back to your first question, your grandfolks don't live by the railroad. They live up in the Kenyontown end of Thurman, like me. That'll be nine, ten miles beyond the station."

As he spoke they rounded a curve and came to the big bridge that spanned the river. The oxen lumbered along steadily, their hoofs clip-clipping across the plank surface. Straight ahead loomed a big lump of a mountain. It looked like a giant artist's palette daubed with autumn hues. There was the pale yellow of popples, cinnamon brown of beech and the oranges and gold of the maples.

"That's called 'Sugarloaf'," Gibby said. "They say the Indians used to call it 'Thunder's Nest.' That's one of the little mountains in the Adirondacks. There's bigger ones where we're going." As he

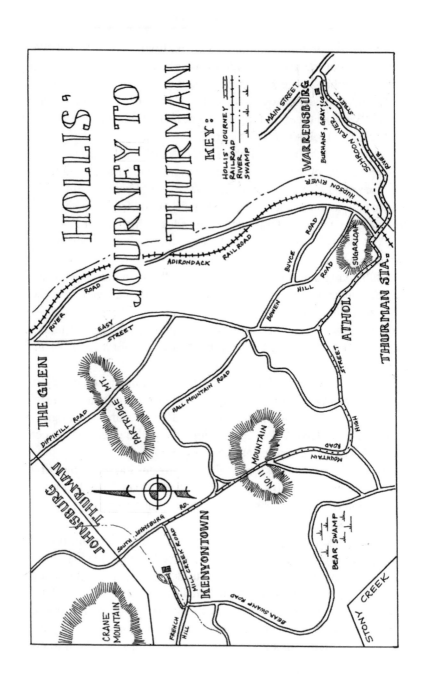

spoke, he guided the oxen around the next curve. Hollis could see the familiar railroad station, a long, homely, rambling building set firmly on a passenger and freight platform. A wooden water tank towered above it, perched on tall wooden legs. Gibby turned into the rail station. Reaching under the wagon seat, he pulled out a heavy pail. "Think you can water the stock while I check the harness?" he asked.

Hollis scrambled to the ground with the big bucket. He had often watered tourists' horses outside the hotel in Warrensburg, sometimes earning a small coin for his trouble. He plunked the bucket down beneath the spigot at the end of the passenger platform and let water flow from the water tank until the bucket overflowed. Bending his knees and bracing himself, he hauled up on the bucket handle. It was too heavy for him to carry with one hand, so he wrapped his arms around the pail and staggered with it toward the wagon.

Gibby turned around just in time to see ice cold water splashing all down Hollis' jacket and trousers. Stifling the impulse to laugh, he watched as the boy allowed each ox in turn to quench its thirst. "You did a good job, son," he said. "That's a big bucket for a lad to tote full. Your grandma and grandpa are sure going to be glad to have your help around the place."

The bucket stowed away once more, the pair climbed back onto the wagon and they were off again, now climbing laboriously uphill out of the fog. Winding clockwise around Sugarloaf Mountain they came to a place where the road leveled out and entered the little settlement of Athol. The sun was climbing high in the sky. Hollis noted with interest a schoolhouse perched on a hill on his left, and then the rough little blacksmith shop where the smithy stilled his rhythmic clanging hammer for a beat and gave Gibby a big wave. Next came the mercantile, with lanterns and wash tubs and boots and calico all crowded into the display windows. The storekeeper, sweeping the porch, called out as they approached, "G'mornin'! You're out and about early today! How's the road holding up?"

"It'll hold up as long as we don't get more rain," Gibby replied with a friendly salute. "Good, good!" the storekeeper said. "Well, now, you have a safe trip."

Gibby assured the man that they would, and drove on past the two-story boarding house, the sawmill with its rasping blades, the gristmill, the crisp white Methodist Church, and then on up the hill out of the hamlet. Despite the sun, the air was chillier here, and Hollis was unable to suppress a shiver.

Gibby reacted quickly. "Why, where's my head? You're soaking wet. Once a man gets wet he can catch a terrible chill." He handed Hollis the reins and wriggled out of his old coat, worn, but lovingly patched. "You put this around you. Your grandmother'll have my head, I bring you home sick!"

He tucked the monstrous coat around Hollis, who felt as though he had taken refuge in a large tent. It was still warm from Gibby's body. "I can't take your coat!" he protested politely.

"Nope, you can't take it," Gibby agreed good naturedly, "but you can use it for a bit. I've got plenty on to keep me warm, and the sun is getting stronger every minute."

And so on they rode, sometimes silent, sometimes chatting amiably. They passed unpretentious little farmhouses with their barns clustered around them like chicks around a hen. Rolling farmland spread out from them in a patchwork of fields—some pasturing small flocks of woolly sheep or placid cows, some bearing the colorful remnants of summer's garden bounty—bright orange pumpkins, blue-green hubbard squashes, mounds of maroon beets or rich tan potatoes. Nearly every dooryard bore signs of fall's wood gathering. Some had stacks of logs to be cut; others had mounds of sawed cordwood tossed in a heap waiting to be split and stacked. Other farmers had their supply already stacked in cords, protected from the weather by woodsheds or by sheets of roofing metal laid across the top and weighted down by rocks. At one house they saw a family hard at work on their wood supply. Two men—Hollis supposed it was a father and his oldest son—rhythmically plied at two-man saw over a log supported by a sawbuck. Each time a chunk dropped to the ground, a boy about Hollis' age scurried to remove it and set it up on its end. Another young man gave each one a well-placed whack with a big axe, splitting it right down the middle. Younger children then ferried the split pieces to a woman, who stacked them in the shed.

They continued to climb higher and higher. Hollis felt hunger chewing at his stomach and glanced behind him to look for his dinner pail. Gibby noted this and correctly guessed the reason.

"I expect we'll be too late for your grandma's dinner—more's the pity—so maybe if you've got a bite to eat in there, you ought to have at it," he said. He knew full well that Hazel Ingraham would have a steaming pot on the back of the stove no matter what time they arrived, but the boy looked as though he hadn't had a decent meal in a long time.

Hollis needed no more encouragement. He opened the bucket and began to devour the johnnycake, his first food in nearly twenty-four hours. Remembering his manners almost too late, he halted abruptly. "Would you care for some?" he asked.

Gibby chuckled. "Son," he said, "I remember what a fine cook your ma is, and I wouldn't normally turn down her baking, but I've got a dinner pail of my own if I get hungry." He continued to smile, but his keen eye did not miss the zeal with which the boy wolfed down every last crumb of the bread. "Come to think of it, I don't believe I'm going to want my dinner, as I had a big breakfast this morning," he lied. "You'd be doing me a favor if you'd eat some from my pail. My ma will skin me alive if I bring it home full."

He nodded toward his own dinner pail behind the seat, and Hollis set in to make short work of the light fluffy biscuits smeared with honey and butter and the generous strips of jerky he found. Full at last, he again turned his attention to the journey. They had just reached the crest of a steep hill, and Gibby stopped the oxen and climbed down. Walking to the rear of the wagon, he took out some rope and began tying the spokes of the rear wheels firmly to a board on the back of the wagon.

"What are you doing?" Hollis asked perplexedly.

"Gotta tie off the wheels for the ride downhill," Gibby explained. "Number Eleven Mountain is too steep to drive the oxen down with the wheels rolling free." He grunted as he pulled the knots taut. "The wagon gets going too fast and runs into the animals. This way, they just drag it down the hill." He climbed back up onto his seat and they made their way down the steep incline. Once they were safely at the bottom, Gibby untied the wheels and they continued their trip.

Hollis again turned his attention to the countryside they traveled through. There were more farmhouses and barns, farmland polka-dotted with rock piles and shocks of corn or buckwheat. High above them, Canada geese circled and honked, debating the wisdom of gliding down to glean the fields. Gibby smacked his lips. "A couple of them would sure dress up a Thanksgiving dinner table!" he said.

As he spoke they came to a crossroads. Hollis saw a small store and a trim white building that had a sign over its door that read "School District # 3." He could hear the rise and fall of voices as children inside recited lessons in unison. He bet they could hardly wait for the school day to be over. A few houses were clustered near the store and school, and a bit further down the road Hollis could see a gleaming white church steeple.

Gibby reined the yoke of oxen to a halt. He gestured broadly at the buildings, and with mock ceremony swept off his hat declaring, "This is Kenyontown."

Hollis' stomach suddenly tied itself into a knot as he realized that this would be where he would be going to school. Would the teacher be mean? Would the other kids like him? How would he fit in? He didn't have long to worry about it, for Gibby shouted, "Haw!" and the oxen swung their heads to the left, turning down the side road.

"You see that mountain there, behind the schoolhouse?" Gibby asked. "That's Crane Mountain, and it stands right beyond your grandfolks' house."

Oh no, they were almost there! Hollis tensed in his seat. Gibby, sensing his fear, began talking again. "You know, the Ingrahams are some of the finest people I know. They're honest, hardworking folks, and they'd share anything they have to help a neighbor in trouble. Life has been hard on them, what with your grandpa's accident and losing your pa so young...." His voice trailed off sadly, and then brightened again. "I'd say having a boy in the house is just what the doctor ordered. You give them a chance and you won't be sorry."

In the short time he had known Gibby, Hollis had already grown to like and trust him, but the prospect of making his home with near strangers filled him with dread. If only he could have stayed with Ma! What would she be doing now? Was she at the hotel?

Once again Gibby called out to the oxen, saying, "Gee!" and reined the oxen onto a side road, this time a narrow lane to the right that was comprised of two well-defined ruts separated by a raggedy strip of grass, all overlaid with a carpet of golden pine needles. Trees lined this roadway, their generous branches arching over it. It began to feel familiar to Hollis, and he recalled traveling down it as a young child, thinking of it as an enchanted tunnel. The wheels of Gibby's wagon settled comfortably into the ruts, and they creaked steadily forward. Moments later they emerged from the trees into a sunny open field and crossed over a small creek. Now to their left Hollis could see a pond, ringed by scruffy willow bushes, swamp alders with their little seed cones dangling from branch tips, red-twigged dogwood and high bush wild cranberries. A pungent wetland odor made Hollis wrinkle his nose. Reflected in the glassy surface of the pond was the autumn blaze of Crane Mountain. They were almost in the Ingraham dooryard before Gibby's voice drew his attention away from the spectacular sight of the pond. "Whoa!" Gibby said, pulling the oxen up short. "We're here, son," he said gently to Hollis.

Hollis' eyes drank in the small clapboard farmhouse, perched on a knoll overlooking the pond. It was freshly painted in the familiar Johnsburg brown. He remembered it. Its door, right in the middle, had a window on either side, like eyes beside a nose, he used to think. The house was trimmed in the color of rich farm cream. An open porch ran across the front of the building and around one side. Above the sloping porch roof, the peaked roof of the house sheltered two more windows. A weathered barn and a handful of small outbuildings stood out beyond the house, with rickety board fences extending from them.

Just then the farmhouse door popped open and a short, wiry woman bustled out onto the porch. "Well, there you are," she exclaimed merrily, "and in good time, too." She stepped quickly off the porch and moved toward the wagon across the muddy yard, instinctively avoiding the puddles. "Hollis, come down off of there.

Let me have a good look at you."

Hollis shucked off Gibby's big coat, climbed down from his seat and awkwardly awaited inspection. His grandmother fussed over him with obvious pleasure, twitching his collar to straighten it, flicking a bit of straw from his lapel and then standing back to take stock of him. "Hollis," she said simply and with great satisfaction.

"Yes, ma'am?" he replied.

"Ma'am? You just call me 'Grandma'. Aren't you turning into a fine young man—a little on the skinny side, but we'll fix that." She stepped forward and pushed a strand of hair back from his face. "You've got your mother's hair, the color of buckwheat in autumn. But, look, you've got your father's eyes! Yes, those are Johnny's eyes, don't you think, Gibby? The same sparkle? And that same stubborn, square jaw." She slipped mistily into memory of another boy of long ago, and then yanked herself back to the present. "Well, come now. Let's get your things inside and get you fed. Gibby, you'll stay and take dinner with us, won't you?"

Gibby, hat in hand, waved off the invitation. "Thanks, but no, Hazel. My folks are expecting me back. Pa needs the wagon for drawing wood."

"Are you sure?" she pressed him. "I put your name in the pot."

"Next time," he promised, and then turned to Hollis, sticking out his big hand. "Hollis, it's been good to meet you."

A wave of dismay swamped Hollis as he watched his new friend prepare to leave. "But—but, I wanted–to thank you, for the ride," he managed lamely.

"My pleasure," Gibby replied. "Maybe if your grandma's agreeable, you'll keep me company another time?"

Hollis nodded eagerly, feeling a little less abandoned as Gibby drove off, leaving him in the care of his grandparents.

3

A New Home

As Hollis' grandmother turned toward the house she said, "Seems like you took a shine to Gibby?" Hollis nodded. "Well, that's as it should be. He's a fine man, come from good stock. His people's place is about a mile up the road, and they're good neighbors. Good neighbors," she repeated for emphasis. "I don't know what we'd have done after your grandfather's accident if it hadn't have been for the Goodnows."

"Where is my..." Hollis hesitated over the unfamiliar title, "my grandfather?"

"Your Grandpa is down fixing some fence out beyond the barns. The cow broke through yesterday and led us on a merry chase, I'll tell you!" She laughed. "It's a pity we didn't have your young legs to help us fetch her home. Yes, it'll be good to have a boy around the place." She paused a moment and then spoke carefully. "Your grandpa won't admit it, but it's hard for him to keep up with the chores, what with his leg and all. It makes him kind of crotchety. That, and other things."

A memory of a white-bearded man flashed into Hollis' mind, a man who sat stone-faced on his wagon seat, and wouldn't come into Ma's house—not the one on River Street, but another house where they had lived before, a house that Hollis barely remembered. He just sat there on the wagon while his wife paid a hasty visit to her grandson and daughter-in-law. Hollis remembered what Ma had said. "They blamed me—things were said...."

Blamed her for what? What could Ma have ever done to turn his grandparents–or perhaps it was only his grandfather–against them? He and Ma had moved away after that visit and had never seen them since.

Poor Ma. It must have been very difficult for her to ask them for help. She must have been desperate. Hollis vowed to himself that he would do everything to make her proud of him. And, he decided, he would find a way to get money for Ma so they could be together again.

Grandma led the way into the little clapboard house, and the steamy odor of baking bread, cinnamon and apples and of simmering ham filled the kitchen into which they stepped. A gleaming black wood stove with shiny nickel trim reigned over the room, a little to the left of center. Three closed doors divided the wall behind it. Off to the right stood a sturdy oak dining table neatly set for four, flanked by a simple pine cabinet. To the left of the stove Hollis could see a low worktable, still snowy with flour from the bread making. A dry sink claimed the sunny spot beneath the side window, and two rockers occupied the space to the left of the door they had entered. There was no plaster ceiling over all this, merely log beams supporting boards that formed the upstairs floors.

Hazel Ingraham waited a moment while Hollis absorbed the scene. "Do you remember this place?" she asked.

"Sort of," he answered, "but it seems smaller."

"You probably don't remember the upstairs at all. You were too little to climb the steps." She led the way to the center door and opened it, revealing a steep, narrow, gray stairway. "Come. I'll show you where to put your things."

Hitching up her long black skirt, she negotiated the steps with surprising agility. She paused at the top of the stairs and gestured to the door on her left. "We have no attic, so this room stores things we don't need every day—my old trunk full of sentimental things, my spinning wheel, things like that."

Turning to the right she led the way around the stairwell, moving down a little hallway toward the front of the house. They had to walk near the stairwell railing to avoid hitting their heads on the ceiling, which sloped sharply down to the left. Grandma opened the door now before them. A white iron bed with lustrous brass trim nearly filled this small bedroom. A quick glance revealed a washstand with a water pitcher, wash bowl and towel rack. A peg-studded board for hanging clothes ran across the tallest wall about a foot below the ceiling, and on the far wall a small window allowed a view of the front yard.

"This used to be our room, your grandfather's and mine, but after he hurt his leg we made the parlor over into a bedroom for us. Now this is a spare room for guests to stay."

She put out a hand to stop Hollis as he started into the room. "Not here. Follow me."

Closing the guestroom door, she opened the last door, revealing a room that in layout was the mirror image of the previous one. "This," she said softly, "was your father's room. I think you should have it." She stepped to one side to allow him to move into the room. Dropping his sack inside the door, he drank in the room that had been his father's, the room that was to be his, from the scrubbed gray floorboards, gaily adorned with a braided rug to the chalky sloped ceiling that seemed to cradle the rich-hued bed beneath it. He ran his fingers over the carved design of vines and leaves that adorned the headboard.

Grandma sat down on the lovingly stitched quilt that covered the bed. "Your grandfather built this bed when your father was just a tadpole. A storm blew down our old cherry tree, so he had it sawed into boards to make furniture. Did the carving and all. We didn't have money to buy a proper spring and mattress, so he wove ropes for the bottom, and I sewed up a cornhusk tick for a mattress." She shifted her weight a little, causing a rustling, crunching noise, and poked her hands down into the makeshift mattress. "Feels like it needs to be re-stuffed, but it'll do for now."

"I don't mind," Hollis said, sitting beside her and bouncing a little on the bed.

"You've got the room with the stovepipe," Grandma continued, pointing to the pipe, which extended about four feet straight up from a metal collar in the floor, and then angled sharply to fit snugly into the side of a half chimney in the corner of his room. "It'll help keep you warm on cold nights." She turned to the dresser. "You can put your clothes in here, and mind you fold them neatly," she instructed. "They're prob'ly all bunched up in that sack."

"Yes, ma'am."

"I'd best be checking on my bread." With that Grandma arose from the bed and started out into the hallway. Immediately she poked her head back into the room. "We'll be eating soon's your grandpa comes in. Scrub up good." And she was gone.

Suddenly exhausted, Hollis sprawled out on the bed, enjoying the sagging of the ropes and the crunching of the cornhusks beneath him.

So much had happened so quickly. This morning he had awakened in his own bed, in his own room in Warrensburg, and now here he was a world away, in a new room, with a new family. And with a mattress that crunched. He tried another little test bounce, but just felt himself sink deeper into the bed. He hoisted himself up and went to the dresser to begin the job of transplanting his scanty wardrobe from the flour sack into the drawers. On top of the dresser he discovered a photograph in a polished wooden frame. In the center was a pretty young woman. Could it be? It was! It was Ma, when she was young. Flanking her were two young men, dressed in their Sunday best. One was husky and jolly-looking—unmistakably Gibby Goodnow. The other, Hollis knew instinctively, was Johnny Ingraham, his father. He saw his own eyes twinkling merrily back at him from the oval frame, his own jaw raised at a stubborn angle, proudly set on some purpose. *What purpose?* Hollis wondered. *To dance with the prettiest girl at Mill Creek?*

He carefully set the picture back on the dresser and began to unpack, remembering his grandmother's instructions. He wasn't a great hand at folding, but he did his best. When he was done, everything he owned was packed into one small drawer. He began to fold the sack when he felt a lump at the bottom. Reaching in he pulled out a few sheets of paper folded around stubby pencil, along with a handkerchief that had some small coins tied up in it. "Write to me!" Ma had said. He put all these things beside his bed so he could begin a letter later.

He turned his attention to the honey-colored pine washstand.

His grandmother had thoughtfully filled the big ironstone pitcher with water for him. He poured some water into the washbasin, and then, carefully putting the pitcher down, he proceeded to splash water on his face. It was cold and he sucked in his breath in a gasp. Grabbing a towel from the washstand rack, he rubbed his face, neck and hands briskly. He was just draping the towel back on the rack

Portrait from the Past

when he heard a clomping on the porch, not the usual tread of a man, but one loud stomp followed by a dragging sound. That would be his grandfather! Hollis blanched as he anticipated meeting him. How would he be received by this man who so resented his mother, this man who blamed Ma for something too terrible to speak about? He hesitated until he heard Grandma open the stairway door and call to him, "Hollis! Come eat!"

He squared his shoulders and bravely marched downstairs. Sanford Ingraham was already seated at the table and scarcely seemed to notice when Hollis slid into the chair his grandmother pointed out to him. The fourth place setting, he noticed, was gone, probably intended for Gibby if he had stayed. Hollis wished he had stayed, to fill the stony silence with his friendly chatter and rumbling laughter.

Grandma tried her best. "San," she said, swishing over from the stove with a platter of boiled ham, "Hollis just got in. Hasn't he grown!"

Sanford Ingraham glanced at Hollis as one might look at an average turnip brought in from the garden. He merely grunted and began carving the ham.

Grandma continued back and forth between the stove and table, relaying dishes of vegetables and steaming hot bread before finally settling into her seat. "Father," she asked, "Will you say grace?"

Hollis bowed his head, sneaking sidelong glances at his grandparents. His grandfather, head bowed and gnarled, rough fingers grasping the edge of the table, began to speak. "God, we thank thee for the bounty on this table today. Let it nourish us so we may do thy work. Amen."

Wordlessly he took up a fork and speared three slices of juicy ham, which he dropped onto Hollis' plate.

"Thank you, sir," Hollis said, his eyes widening as Grandma then added a heap of fluffy mashed potatoes and a pile of green beans. Somehow he managed to find a spot to squeeze in a slab of fresh bread slathered in butter.

"You be sure to try some of my whortleberry jam on that," Grandma said, pushing the glass of fruit spread toward him.

"Yes, ma'am. Thank you," he said.

"'Grandma', remember?" she prompted. "And he's 'Grandpa'," she added.

"Yes, ma'am. Grandma, I mean," he corrected himself awkwardly.

She laughed. "It'll take some getting used to, I expect," she said. Then, turning her attention to her husband, she asked, "You still slaughtering over to Websters' this afternoon, being as it's late?"

Grandpa didn't glance up from the plate he was steadily and systematically emptying. "Yup. He's just got the one hog this year. Shouldn't take long. Be home 'bout dark."

"Perhaps Hollis could go along and give you a hand," she suggested.

This time the old man looked up. "Now what do you suppose a town boy knows about helping slaughter hogs?" he asked pointedly.

Grandma's response was soft, but equally pointed. "What does any boy know about anything till someone teaches him?" she asked.

Hollis held his breath, wondering what would happen.

His grandfather merely grunted and said, "He can come or he can stay, as he pleases."

Hollis struggled to sound self-assured, but managed only to squeak out, "I'd like to go." Actually, he wasn't at all sure he wanted to go, but somehow being called a "town boy" seemed like a challenge that required him to go.

Grandma appeared glad, so he guessed he'd made the right choice. "I'd just like you to fill up the kindling box and bring me in a pail of water before you go," she said.

As soon as dinner was over, crowned with hot cinnamon-y apple pie, Hollis set about these chores, working under Grandma's tutelage. Grandpa settled on the porch; carefully plying a whetstone over two knives, stopping from time to time to test their sharpness by drawing the blade lightly across his thumbnail. Satisfied at last, he laid the knives on a soft piece of leather, which he folded over them. He rolled up the leather and tied the bundle with a piece of rawhide and deposited it with some other items in a pail on the porch. Then he went to the barn to harness the horses for the trip. He pulled the wagon into the yard just as Hollis was carrying in the

last armload of firewood. Hurriedly dumping the wood into the
wood box, Hollis started for the wagon.

"Wait!" Grandma called. "Your grandfather will be needing that
pail of tools on the porch. And this," she said, handing him a rifle.

Gingerly taking the gun, he picked up the pail of tools and
joined his grandfather on the wagon. Grandma, who had followed
him out, handed Hollis a pie covered with a starched red and white
tea towel. "San, you give this to Sylvia Webster. Tell her I baked
extra because I thought Gibby was coming to dinner, and she'd be
doing me a favor keeping it from going to waste."

Grandpa nodded, snapped the lines over the team, and they set
off. They retraced the route across the meadow and out through the
tunnel, but this ride was certainly different from Hollis' ride with
Gibby. Too timid to begin a conversation with his grandfather, the
boy rode in silence broken only by the steady clop-clop of the horses' hoofs. Hollis sneaked a look at his grandfather, and saw a proud
man who sat straight and tall on the wagon seat. His eyes were clear
and bright, and his jaw, Hollis realized with surprise, had, under the
bristling white beard, the same squareness as the young man in the
photo. Time and something else—was it pain?—had set deep lines
around his eyes and mouth, in the skin that looked like coarse
tanned leather.

They turned south onto the Mill Creek Road and hadn't gone
very far when they crested a small hill. At the foot of the hill Hollis
could see a forlorn cluster of weathered buildings huddled beside a
creek next to the road. Two men were feeding a fire under a huge
black kettle in the back yard. Grandpa halted the team and turned
to Hollis, addressing him directly for the first time.

"That's Bob Webster," he said. His voice took on a sharper tone
when he added, "That's his brother-in-law Ike Watson with him."
He paused and then asked, "You ever been to a slaughtering?"

Hollis shook his head.

"It's not a pretty sight. There's the road home if you want it."

Was his grandfather offering him a way out? Hollis glanced at
him. There was no softening of his harsh features as he sat staring
straight ahead. No, he was probably hoping Hollis would chicken
out and prove him right about "town boys." Hollis straightened up

in his seat. "Nope," he said firmly, "I'm going."

"So be it," Grandpa said, clucking to the team.

4

The Hog Slaughtering

They continued down the hill and across the creek to the dreary little house where the Websters lived. At the sound of their arrival, the door of the house burst open and a handful of tow-headed youngsters scattered from it like startled partridges. Grandpa lowered himself stiffly from the wagon, motioning to Hollis to wait. "Hand me down that bucket, first. That's right. Now the rifle. Mind how you point that."

As Hollis carefully extracted the gun from under the seat and passed it down, he discovered that the Webster children had formed a semicircle around the wagon and were staring up at him, their enormous blue eyes wide with curiosity. The oldest boy, whom Hollis judged to be about his own age, blurted out the question on all their minds. "Who are you?"

"Name's Hollis," he replied.

"Mine's Tommy," the boy said and, pointing at his siblings one by one, added, "and this here's Charlotte, and Clarence, and Lulu, and Lila and Baby Emmett.

Hollis nodded politely. "My grandmother sent your mother this pie," he began, as he handed the pie to Tom. "She said—" There was no opportunity to finish the explanation, for Tommy immediately disappeared into the house with the pie, followed like the pied piper by the younger children. Hollis shrugged, clambered down and picked up the bucket of tools. He hurried to catch up with Grandpa, who was headed out behind the house. A heavyset balding man hung back and eyed them sullenly while a thin wiry man with a scraggly beard hurried out to greet them.

"Afternoon, Sanford," he said, wiping his hands on his dirty tattered breeches and reaching out to shake the man's hand. "And who's the lad?" he asked, looking at Hollis.

"Hollis," Grandpa said abruptly, "come from Warrensburg."

"Good, good. The more the merrier," the man said agreeably. He nodded his head toward the bald man. "Ike—you know Ike—come to give a hand, too."

Leading the way, Bob Webster pointed out a black and white hog switching his tail and grunting nonchalantly in a pen in the rear of the dark, smelly barn. "Just have one this year, and he's so small it don't hardly make sense to do 'im, but what am I gonna do? Kids gotta eat somethin' asides beans once in a while. And I sure can't afford to feed a hog through the winter."

Grandpa nodded sympathetically. "It was a short growing season. Not much extra to fatten hogs on," he said.

"Or children," Mr. Webster said, stroking his beard anxiously. Then, returning to the job at hand, he asked Grandpa, "Where do you want 'im?"

Grandpa looked around. "Here's as good as anywhere." He carefully unwrapped his knives and laid them out on the flat top rail of the pigpen. Picking up the rifle, he loaded it and stepped inside the pen, latching the gate behind him.

"Let's be done with it," he said.

He raised the muzzle of the gun and trained it on the forehead of the pig. Hollis held his breath in dread as the pig raised its head to examine the barrel of the gun, amiably grunting and sniffing. Grandpa's finger was slowly drawing back the trigger when a derisive snort behind him caused the pig to jerk his head away. Grandpa lowered the gun.

It was Ike Watson, who had followed them in from the yard. "Well, I've heerd of it, but I ain't ever seed it afore—a man wasting a bullet on a hog!" He spat a long stream of brown spittle on the barn floor.

Hollis could see irritation on Grandpa's face, but the old man said nothing. Bob Webster fidgeted in embarrassment.

Ike Watson was oblivious to their reaction. "I allus say," he continued, "the only way to do in a hog is to whack it good atween the ears with a shovel or a sledge and then stick it with the knife. That's how you get a good bleed."

Grandpa straightened up and turned to glare at Ike, but Bob hastened to smooth things over. "Different folks does things different," he said.

"I can speak for myself," Grandpa said. He kept his voice even, but Hollis could hear the annoyance in it. "I've been butchering hogs the better part of fifty years and I've never felt it necessary to whack a hog with a shovel. I use one bullet to the center of the forehead to drop the pig and then I stick it. True," he continued with a note of sarcasm in his voice, "my hogs don't run around the yard spraying blood all over until they die, but I never had a one that didn't bleed out just fine all the same."

"That's true," Bob said nervously. "His hogs allus bleeds out good, Ike."

Ike spat again, glaring at Bob. "It's your hog," he said.

Turning back to the pig, Grandpa raised the rifle again. This time there was no interruption. Hollis heard the sudden loud crack of the gun, and the hog, looking slightly surprised, crumpled onto the floor. Hollis had known it was coming, but he was stunned all the same. One minute the pig was alive, and the next minute he was dead. Just like that.

Grandpa wasted no time. Leaning the rifle against the slats of the pen, he grabbed one of the hog's forelegs. Bob entered the pen and seized the hind legs, and together they rolled the pig onto its back. Grandpa selected one of the knives from the railing and, plunging the knife into one side of the hog's neck, ripped it sideways to the other jowl. The hog made a funny gurgling noise, and blood foamed from the gash, releasing into the air a hot, sweet stench.

It all happened so swiftly that Hollis felt as if he were floating in some grisly dream. The horror of the scene gushed over him in throbbing waves. He was stunned to see the matter-of-fact manner of those around him. Even the Webster children, bellies now full of pie, were all lined up along the wooden slats of the pen, exchanging observations about the amount of blood and how fast the pig had dropped.

Before he realized it, Hollis was bolting from the barn in a desperate race against the nausea welling up in his throat. He just made it around the corner of the barn before wave after wave of vomiting overcame him. Finally through, he leaned weakly against the barn, suddenly aware that, once again, he was encircled by Webster children, staring saucer-eyed at him. It was Lulu who broke the silence by racing back into the barn, shouting at the top of her lungs, "Pa, that boy is puking all over everywhere!"

Hollis could hear Ike Watson's nasty haw-hawing. "Well, seems like yore boy don't have much taste for hog's blood, neither!"

Hollis was mortified. It was one thing to make a fool of himself, but to embarrass his grandfather was unacceptable. He broke through the ring of giggling children. He wanted to disappear off the face of the earth, and thought briefly of running. He could run down the lane, across the bridge, down Mill Creek Road. He could keep running until he was home in Warrensburg. But no, that would be just what Sanford Ingraham expected him to do, and wanted him to do. He wouldn't give him the satisfaction.

Wiping his mouth on his sleeve, he strode resolutely back into the barn. Without looking up, Grandpa kicked some straw over the pool of blood, took his knife and made a vertical slit between the bone and tendon in the back of each of the hog's hind legs. Then Bob and Ike slipped large hooks into the slits. Without ceremony they dragged the hog out of the barn to a makeshift table set up a few feet from the iron kettle, now steaming vigorously. Grandpa picked up his knife and wiped it with a handful of clean straw from the pen floor. He motioned to Hollis to bring the bucket of tools, and together they followed the others.

Bob and Ike heaved the pig up onto the table. "Tom!" Bob barked. "Bring me them burlap sacks around the side of the shed."

Tom disappeared, returning shortly with an armful of sacks. Bob had more instructions. "Get me two, three candlesticks from the barn and that sack of rosin."

The Hog

Tom returned from this errand and Grandpa reached into his pail, saying, "I've brought a couple of candlesticks, too." He handed the surprised Hollis an instrument that looked sort of like a circular school bell with a wooden handle sticking up. Bob took rosin from the sack and began rubbing it into the bristly hair of the hog. Grandpa draped the pig with burlap bags, and Bob soaked them down with pails of boiling water he had scooped out of the kettle. They let the scalding hot water do its work, and then removed one of the bags. Grandpa wrapped his fingers around the handle of his candlestick and began working the "bell" part of it in circles around the pig's hide, scraping off the bristly hair. Hollis moved closer and followed his example, and was soon joined by Tom, Ike and Bob. Every so often one of the men would dip a pail of water out of the kettle and pour it over the area they were working on to clean off the hair and dirt they had scraped free and loosen more. As each area was completed, they peeled off another bag and continued until the first side was done.

Hollis was amazed to discover that his horror of the slaughter was almost erased by the camaraderie of working shoulder to shoulder with the men. They followed the same procedure on the other side of the carcass. They worked quickly, and in no time the pig was clean and free of hair.

The men threaded an iron bar into the slits in the hind legs, and with the help of a pulley and some stout rope, hung the hog head down from a nearby tree limb.

Tom then dragged a much-battered galvanized tub across the ground and placed it almost under the hog, while Grandpa produced another of his knives and skillfully began plying it along the pig's underside. As he completed the cut that ran from between the pig's hindquarters all the way to its chin, he stepped back and leaned against the work table. The two younger men moved in and pulled the two sides of the pig apart, revealing all its internal organs, which, no longer held in place by muscles and ribs, began to sag. Grandpa again stepped in and deftly slid the knife around the body cavity, releasing the organs so they slithered in a smelly heap into the tub. Tom jabbed Hollis, who was staring wide-eyed, and said, "C'mon. Help me drag the guts out."

Hollis followed his lead and grabbed one of the handles of the tub to help drag it out of the way. "Where do you dump it?" he asked.

Tom straightened up and looked at him in amazement. "Don't you know anything?" he demanded rudely. "Ma and Charlotte gotta go through it first. For the heart and liver and casings and such. There's a lot comes outta that tub before it gets throwed anywhere. And when we're all done, we even rake up the bristles to use in plastering."

Ike, hearing this exchange, laughed his sneering laugh and said, "Boy don't know much about farm life, does he?"

Sanford Ingraham merely grunted, and Hollis, his cheeks burning with embarrassment, silently vowed not to do anything else to belie his "town boy" upbringing.

Once the body cavity of the pig was cleaned out, Mrs. Webster appeared, and just as Tom had predicted, she and Charlotte began rooting through the guts, extracting the usable organs and placing them in big basins for washing. Mrs. Webster remarked about what a big heart it was, and how good it would taste at dinner the next day.

The men rinsed off their candlesticks and knives, and left the hog hanging from the tree to cool. Hollis took the bucket of tools and rifle to place in the wagon while Grandpa said his good-byes to the Websters and, Hollis assumed, collected his pay. Hollis decided not to draw any further attention to himself, and just climbed up onto the wagon seat for the dreaded ride home. What would his grandfather have to say about his awful display of weakness? Would he say he was disappointed? No, Hollis guessed, Grandpa probably had expected no better from him. He slumped miserably on the seat, too embarrassed to even try to apologize. Grandpa joined him and they started off, traveling without conversation for some time.

Finally Hollis could bear the silence no longer. "It was awful," he blurted out. "I could never kill pigs, no matter how much money they paid me," he said.

"Money!" Grandpa said in disbelief. "I don't get money for slaughtering hogs."

Hollis' amazement showed in his face. "You do that for free?"

Grandpa's answers were short, almost sarcastic. "Not for free. Bob Webster 'paid' me last summer when he helped me skid out logs and saw them into firewood. Or maybe they 'paid' me when Miz Webster came down to nurse your Grandma when she was feeling poorly last winter. We aren't like town people. Folks out here don't have much money. They 'pay' each other with help when it's needed, or a spare sack of potatoes or a pie or such."

"Well, how do you earn money, then?" Hollis asked, trying to grasp the idea.

"Don't have much need of money out here," Grandpa said. "We grow most of what we need, and what we can't grow we usually trade for. It's the country way."

"But what if you do need money?" Hollis persisted.

"Well, sometimes we grow what you call a 'cash crop', like an extra field of hay or buckwheat or potatoes to sell in town. Or some make barrel hoops to sell to the mills, or draw loads with their wagons." His grandfather looked at him more closely then. "It's town people that set such a store by money. What's it good for?"

Hollis hesitated, unsure how much his grandfather knew about his mother's situation, and equally unsure how much he wanted this man–who didn't approve of his mother–to know. "Oh, I don't know," he said, trying to sound casual, "like for rent or something." The conversation wasn't going well, but Hollis really needed to know more, so he asked, "Do you grow a cash crop?"

"Used to. No more," Grandpa said tersely. Hollis noticed that grimness had returned to his face. They finished their ride in silence.

When they arrived back at the farmhouse, Grandma hurried out into the semidarkness to bring them a gleaming lantern. "I already slopped the hogs and took care of the chickens, " she said, "but the rest of the animals are waiting for you." Grandpa began unhitching the team, and Hollis, unwilling to seem ignorant of country ways, watched for ways to help, and carefully gathered up the harness to hang in the barn. He helped put the horses up in their stalls.

"Well, you're here," Grandpa said tersely. "Might as well learn the ropes." He sent Hollis up to the loft to fork hay down to the floor below. As he pitched the sweet-smelling clover and timothy, he could hear a gentle murmuring. He paused for a moment and heard Grandpa's surprising gentleness as he gave the team a brisk rubdown. "There, there Gwen. That's a good girl. Do you need a little liniment on that back leg? Whoa, Jackie, your turn is coming. Easy, boy." Without saying a word, Hollis climbed down the loft ladder. Grandpa directed him to fork a pile of the fresh hay into the mangers of Gwen and Jackie and do the same for the brown Jersey cow he called Jessie, placidly chewing her cud in a pen next to Gwen and Jackie. Next he gave each of them a scoop of grain. "Maggie has had her slops," Grandpa said. "Just give her a little corn." Hollis found the barrel of shelled corn and gave the young sow a scoop. Lastly Hollis took hay and feed to the half dozen or so silly sheep that milled around a pen at the end of the barn.

By the time he had finished that job, Grandpa had groomed the horses and cleaned out their hooves and had begun to milk Jessie. He directed Hollis to fetch water from the creek for the stock. Hollis obediently picked up one of the pails hanging neatly beside the barn door.

"Take two," Grandpa said. "They'll balance you." Two buckets! It had been all he could do to manage one bucket for Gibby's oxen, so how in the world could he carry two? Hollis privately fumed, but he was determined to show Grandpa that he was as good as any farm boy. He grabbed a second bucket and headed down the short, well-worn path to the creek. He filled the buckets just full enough so they wouldn't spill as he walked, and hoisted them up. He could barely carry them, but he gritted his teeth and made his way toward the barn, stopping only once to set them down for a moment before delivering them to the animals. By the time he had made the necessary three trips to the creek, his arms felt like they were going to drop off. Reentering the barn for the last time, Hollis drank in the sweet smells–the mixture of milk, yesterday's clover, molasses-coated grain, the grassy breath of the cow and the sweat of the horses.

Grandpa had finished the milking and had just returned from shutting up the chicken coop for the night. He handed Hollis the pail of fresh, creamy milk, and silently closed the barn door and turned toward the house. The sharp scent of wood smoke lay in the

air, and they made their way to the little house with lantern light
streaming from its windows. Hollis adjusted his pace to the dragging limp of his grandfather. They stopped on the porch to wash up,
each working the pump handle while the other lathered up with
strong-smelling lye soap and rinsed away the work of the day.

Warmth from the stove enveloped them when they entered the
house. Grandma looked up from her work and wiped her hands on
her apron. "There you are! Go back out and stamp the dirt off of
those boots, then come in and take off your coats and set. I've fixed
you a nice supper."

They sat as directed, and Grandma brought over a platter heaped
with cold slices of ham. Visions of the dead pig and the steaming
blood and guts invaded Hollis' senses and he abruptly pushed himself away from the table, saying, "'Scuse me. I'm not hungry." He
practically raced up the stairs, followed by Grandma's puzzled
stare.

"Now what's got into that boy?" she asked.

Hollis could hear his grandfather reply, "Tired, I expect. He's
not used to farm work."

He guessed Grandpa was too embarrassed to tell even Grandma
about how he'd behaved that afternoon, but suspected Grandma
would get at the truth eventually. He felt his way down the dark hall
to his bedroom, where his grandmother had left a lamp burning low.
He sat on the bed, waiting for his stomach to settle. He was very
tired, he realized. He stood up to get a nightshirt from the bureau,
and, as he neared the stovepipe, his grandparents' voices, until now
just a murmuring sound, became clear. Hearing Grandpa speak his
name, he could not resist stopping to listen.

"He's a good boy," Grandma responded to whatever he had said.

"He doesn't belong here," Grandpa said firmly.

"Where else would he belong, but with kin?" Grandma bristled.

"He belongs with his Ma," Grandpa said. "Mary's made her bed,
she can lie in it."

"Why, what would you have her do? Stand out on the street with
a tin cup? She's doing the best she knows how to make a life for her
and the boy."

Grandpa snorted derisively. "The best she knows! All she knows is money. It's money that's got her in this fix. She and Johnny never should have gone off like that, and I know it was all her doing. Well, look where it's got them. Look where it's got our Johnny. Her always wanting money."

"So we're back to that again. It's always that, and I've always disagreed with you. There has to be another explanation, but you never gave her a chance to explain."

Grandpa's voice raised a notch. "What's to explain? It was clear—she wanted town life, first North Creek, then Warrensburg. Town life, and town things. Now the boy is paying for her foolishness. He's got money on his mind. I figure he's wanting to get some money to help pay her debts. And him only a young tad and away from his ma. The parent ought to stay with the child, money or no money!"

Now Grandma's voice raised. "Like you stayed with Johnny and me? I begged you to stay, but no, you had to go off to that logging camp to earn extra money."

Hollis heard Grandpa's fist thump the table. "Hazel, you know we needed money for the new sugarhouse. Now it's been years, and you've never forgiven me for coming home from that log drive a cripple, have you? There, I've said it—a cripple! A cripple with a shriveled up, worthless leg, half the man I was when I left!"

"San," Grandma said, her voice softer now, "when you came back I was so glad to see you, I would have forgiven you anything. It's not the crippled leg that's come between us, it's the way it's soured you and made you hard. And what the accident started, losing our Johnny finished. Well, now we have Johnny's son, and it's like a new beginning for us. Don't shut yourself off from it. Please."

Hollis, feeling guilty for eavesdropping, took a step toward the bureau. He winced as a floorboard creaked under him. Grandpa cleared his throat loudly, and Grandma suddenly began clattering the supper dishes.

Hollis quickly changed his clothes and slipped into bed. He was about to blow out the lamp when he spotted the paper and pencil. Ma would be wanting to hear from him, but what could he write? He wrote carefully, "Dear Ma," and put the pencil down. What next? *Today we killed a pig and it was horrible and I threw up.*

Grandpa doesn't want me here. He doesn't like you. He's really mad. Hollis picked up the pencil again and began to write. "I got here fine and I am being good. I helped Grandpa with chores. Everything is fine." He put the paper and pencil back on the nightstand. That was enough for one night; he would add more tomorrow.

He blew out the lamp and snuggled down under the covers that smelled of lye soap and crisp starch. His body hollowed out a little nest in the cornhusk tick. He tried to understand all that he had just heard. Ma? Wanting "town things?" Ma never seemed to want anything for herself, just food, a roof over their heads and to owe nothing to anybody. That was the Ma that he knew. Grandpa was wrong. He pounded his pillow angrily. It felt so good, he did it again. That sour old man was wrong. The Sour Man. That was a good name for him, Hollis thought. He rolled over to look out the window.

The moon clearly illuminated the graceful arcs of Crane Mountain proudly defining the horizon. He was still gazing at the mountain when his eyes, overcome by exhaustion, drooped into sound, dreamless sleep.

5

Farm Life

Hollis was jolted back to wakefulness by a loud banging on the floor, right beneath his head. He rubbed his eyes, trying to figure out where he was. He could hear Grandma's laughter as she said, "Sanford, you just put up that broomstick!"

Again there came a bang, bang, bang! "You gonna sleep all day, boy? Your grandma's got a stack of buckwheat cakes big enough to choke a horse. You'd better get down here before I eat 'em all!"

Hollis lost no time scurrying into his clothes, and was about to hurry downstairs when his Grandmother shouted, "And don't forget to wash up!"

When he appeared at the table, properly scrubbed, Grandma nodded approval and slid a plateful of buckwheat cakes, dripping with butter, under his chin. "There's honey in the pot and jam in the jar. Help yourself," she offered.

Hollis needed no further invitation. He spread the pancakes with thick honey and dug in.

Finally he came up for air and managed to say, "These are good."

Grandma stood with her hands on her hips, smiling broadly. "My, it does my heart good to see a boy with a healthy appetite!" she declared.

"My ma makes pancakes sometimes," Hollis said, wiping a

sticky spot on his chin with his napkin. "We used to put maple syrup on them."

Grandma's smile evaporated and she turned quickly away and began fussing with the stove. Grandpa pushed his plate away, leaving two uneaten sausages, and stood up abruptly. "Got lots of chores this morning," Grandpa said, and went out onto the porch. Hollis wondered what he had done or said wrong, but didn't dare ask.

Chores began right after breakfast. As the Sour Man had promised, there were a lot of them. First there were the barn chores, although this time he didn't have to haul water for any of the big stock, as they were turned out of the barn for the day, and could walk to the creek to drink. Hollis took water to the chickens and gathered eggs from the nesting boxes. He cleaned the floor and spread around a little fresh hay. Next he returned to the barn. Setting down the eggs, he went to work cleaning out the animals' stalls, following Grandpa's terse instructions. He was determined that the old man would never have to tell him anything twice or correct him, so he made sure to listen closely. After carrying the last forkful of the droppings and waste hay out to the manure pile in the barnyard, he spread out fresh bedding. Grandpa finished the milking and turned the cow out into the barnyard. Picking up the milk, he started for the house. Hollis picked up the egg basket, closed the barn door and followed.

If Hollis had thought he was going to get away without hauling water that morning, he was sadly mistaken. First he pumped water into the water pitchers for the bedrooms and carried in buckets of water for the reservoir on the wood stove, where it was heated for dishwashing and such.

Next, Grandma led him around to the side of the house where a large barrel was carefully positioned to catch any rainwater that might drip off the roof. "Dip your bucket in here," she said, "and bring in enough bucketfuls to fill my copper boiler in the kitchen. We've got clothes to wash, and rainwater does the best job."

While Grandma was separating the milk, he hauled buckets of the soft rainwater to her big oblong copper boiler on the stove and carried wood for the fire to heat it. Then more water had to be hauled to the galvanized tub on the floor next to the stove, where

Grandma would scrub the clothes. By the time he was done, his arms ached and his fingers had big blisters. He didn't mind much, though. He could see from the way that Grandma was looking at him that he was doing a good job, and that pleased him.

Grandma shaved a block of lye soap into the boiler and deposited the white clothes. While the water heated, Grandma went to her chair on the porch and whirled the handle of her small glass and metal churn and supervised Hollis as he dragged big baskets of vegetables in from the garden. There were bushels of potatoes, squashes, turnips, carrots and parsnips to be kept in cool dark bins in a corner of the cellar. "Leave those cabbages, tomatoes, peppers and onions right in the corner of the kitchen," Grandma said. "I'll be starting my sauerkraut soon and putting up my end-of-the-garden relish." She showed him how to split kindling, and he refilled the wood box, and then he helped her carry the bowl of butter to the cool basement to chill. They poured the milk into a covered metal pail and carefully lowered it into the well to stay fresh.

Then it was time to begin the laundry. The tub of white clothes was now near boiling. With a big paddle-like stick, Grandma stirred and pounded the clothes, and then, still using the paddle, lifted each garment from the steaming boiler and deposited it in the galvanized tub to cool a bit. She vigorously rubbed the clothes over her scrub board, rubbing some skin off her knuckles as she did so. She set Hollis to work cranking the soggy clothes through a wringer and placing them in a second empty tub. When all the white clothing had been taken from the boiler, Grandma and Hollis lifted it down off the stove and allowed the water to cool before Grandma put in the dark clothes, like Grandpa's trousers, and began the process all over again.

Finally all were washed, and Hollis and Grandma lugged the boiler out onto the porch and dumped the dirty water onto the ground. Hollis carried buckets of fresh water in, and they rinsed the clothes and wrung them out again. Grandma studied the sky, which had been filling with clouds all morning. A chilly breeze was stirring. "I guess I'll chance it and hang them out awhile. It's going to rain, but maybe the breeze will at least start them drying." Their fingers were numb by the time the last pair of trousers was clipped to the clothesline, but still the job was not completed. Grandma had Hollis carry buckets of the used rinse water and splash it over the porch floorboards while she energetically plied her broom over them, making them sparkling clean. They hung the galvanized tubs and copper boiler on nails sticking out of the side of the house. Then they hurried into the house, quickly shutting the door behind them and huddling beside the stove.

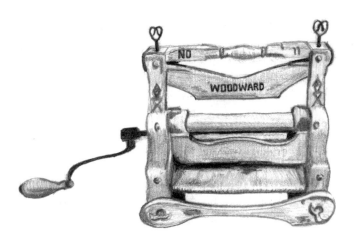

The Wringer

"Brrr!" Grandma exclaimed, stuffing another log into the firebox of the stove. "Those clothes prob'ly won't dry out there. This afternoon we'll have to bring them in here and hang them around to finish drying." She peered out the window toward the barn. "Now what do you suppose is keeping your grandfather down to the barn so long? His leg will be achin' something awful after being out in this cold."

Hollis took this opportunity to satisfy his curiosity. "How did Grandpa hurt his leg?" he asked.

"It happened a long time ago," she answered, "when your father was a few years older than you. Your pa and grandpa had a dream. Your grandpa was known all over for making the best maple syrup around. He was tapping quite a lot of trees, but there were plenty more waiting to be tapped. With your pa old enough to help, Grandpa thought they could hang out lots more buckets and tap all the sugar bush. Then they could boil down lots of syrup and sell it down in Saratoga Springs. But first they decided they needed to build a decent sugarhouse to do the boiling in. She wiped her hands on her apron and smiled fondly. "Oh, you should have seen those two! They were like two boys, putting their heads together figuring it all out. Well, your grandpa decided the only way they could get the money ahead for the sugarhouse was if he went off to Newcomb and worked the winter at a lumber camp."

"And so that's what he did?" Hollis asked with interest.

"Yes. No amount of arguing on my part would sway him; he would do it. So off he went that November, to be returning in May. But it didn't work out the way he planned. When the men were driving the logs down river in the spring, he and two others were sent out in a boat to break up a jam in mid-river. They broke it up, all right, but they weren't able to get clear before the logs came rushing down at them. Their boat was swamped. Your grandpa's leg was crushed between two logs, and he was nearly drowned before his comrades on shore were able to fish him from the water." She was silent for a moment, then added, "And he was the lucky one. The other two were lost. Their bodies weren't found for weeks. Two good men!"

Grandma began to poke the fire vigorously. "Hollis, go down to the barn and see what's keeping that man."

Hollis wanted to ask if they had ever built the sugarhouse, but Grandma continued before he could ask. "I'll be putting dinner on directly, so tell him to come on. Oh, and tell him to bring up those butternuts from the barn. We'll work on those this afternoon."

Obediently Hollis headed for the barn, turning up his coat collar against the biting wind. Grandpa was just emerging from the barn with a pail when he got there. "Grandma says to come on up for dinner now. And she says we're to bring up the butternuts."

"Figured she'd be wantin' 'em," Grandpa said, holding up the bucket in his hand. Hollis took the bucket of big, fuzzy, green-brown nuts while Grandpa bolted the barn door with an ash stick worn glossy smooth by years of use. Hollis noticed that he leaned briefly against the side of the barn as if bracing himself for the walk back to the house. They walked slowly, Hollis carrying the bucket and Grandpa dragging his crushed leg.

"Kick the dirt off your boots," he said as they reached the porch. "Your grandmother'll skin you alive, you track mud on her clean floors."

Grandma had stew and hot biscuits waiting for them when they arrived, and she filled the dinnertime conversation with talk about the morning's accomplishments. If Grandpa heard her praise of Hollis' hard work, he gave no sign. Finally she asked, "You going back down to the barn after dinner to mend harness?"

He nodded, "I want to mend the fly net before I put it up for the winter. The horses will be needing it come spring plowing."

"If you don't need Hollis, I'll have him help me hull the butternuts," Grandma said. "I've been wanting to dye that new batch of wool so I can get to knitting."

Hollis didn't know what butternuts had to do with knitting, but after dinner he found out. Grandma set him up by the stove with a block of wood and a hammer, and, one by one, he split the leathery outer covering of each nut, separating it from the woody inner shell. He liked the sharp smell of the rind and marveled at the dark brown juice that oozed from it and stained his fingers. She watched him for a moment as he worked, then touched his shoulder. "Many's the time your father sat just like that, hulling butternuts for me. He was a good worker, just like you." Into a huge pot of steaming water went the pieces of hull, rapidly turning it a deep shade of brown.

"There," Grandma pronounced when the last hull was swimming, "that'll make a fine batch of dye! While that's simmering, let's you and me go fetch the yarn out of the storeroom. We'll leave the nuts to crack another day." She placed the pail of nuts in the little pantry off the kitchen, and led the way up the steep steps, her skirts rustling briskly. "You haven't seen the storeroom, have you?" she asked, opening the door.

Hollis picked his way through the room crowded with treasures-
an old leather-bound trunk, a spinning wheel, a straw bonnet and a
tattered umbrella. Up near the ceiling a fine string was stretched
from one end of the room to the other. Threaded onto the string
were "leather britches," string beans hung to dry for cooking during the winter. All along the left wall from floor to ceiling ran
shelves. Some were filled with neatly arranged jars of dried herbs.
Some sported piles of carefully folded swatches of colorful fabric.

"Those are pieces I'm saving for my next quilt," Grandma said,
catching his glance. "Over there," she said, gesturing toward baskets overflowing with larger fabric pieces, "those pieces are to cut
up for my rug making."

Just then Hollis spied, on the topmost shelf, the neck of a violin
protruding. Grandma, following his gaze, took it down and, almost
tenderly, stroked away the dust with the corner of her apron. "That
was your grandpa's fiddle," she said. "My, how he could make it
sing! Used to be he was called on to play at all the husking bees and
kitchen hops." She smiled at the happy memories.

"Doesn't he play it anymore?" Hollis asked.

"Oh, no," Grandma said. "He hasn't played it since—" A cloud
came over her face, and she stopped. "Well, he just doesn't play it
anymore. Anyhow, it's broken," she concluded lamely, as if that
would explain why Grandpa no longer played the fiddle. She
replaced the fiddle upon the shelf and turned her thoughts to the
business at hand. "Well, we came up here for wool, and there it is.
Grab that basket and let's go back downstairs."

Hollis picked up the basket of yarn and the two returned to the
kitchen where Grandma began dying the bundles of thick nubby
yarn in the butternut solution, turning it from dingy white to rich
tan.

"I've got only a few more skeins to go," she said after awhile.
"You'd better go bring in those clothes from outside so they can be
drying by the stove."

"Sure, Grandma," he said, pulling on his coat and heading outside. The clothes, unable to dry in the moisture-laden air, were still
sodden. He yanked off the clothespins and dropped the heavy, wet
mess into Grandma's laundry basket. By the time he plopped in the

last pair of trousers, there was a small mountain of clothes. Reluctant to stay out in the cold a moment longer than necessary, he wrestled the basket off the ground and began lurching toward the house with it. He staggered up the porch steps and lunged for the doorknob, loosening his grasp on the basket as he did so. The pile of clothes began to cascade to the porch floor, so he quickly tipped the basket back in the other direction. The clothing then began to topple off the other side of the basket. The more he tried to right it, the worse the situation became. There was no hope for it now, but Hollis rode it out to the end, staggering first this way, and then that way, until the whole swaying pile landed in a soggy heap on the porch, with him plopped unceremoniously in the middle of it.

A low coughing noise caused him to jerk his head around. There was Grandpa, covering his mouth with his hand as he continued his odd strangled coughing. It sounded almost as though he were laughing, but Hollis knew that was not possible, for the Sour Man never even smiled, let alone laughed.

His coughing subsided and Grandpa said in his usual stern voice, "Your Grandma'll skin you alive, you get those clothes dirty." The door opened then, and there stood Grandma, arms akimbo, surveying the scene in amazement. "Why didn't you holler?" she asked, laughing. "What a sight you are! Both of you!" she added, looking much happier than you'd expect of a woman whose clean laundry was strewn all over the porch.

Together the three of them gathered up the clothes and carried them into the toasty warm kitchen where Grandma supervised their re-hanging on a network of lines she had strung. "There," she said when all was done, "they're unsightly and in the way, but they'll dry. And now, young man," she said with mock severity, "I'd say you're about due for a washing, too!"

Hollis was mystified. He knew this house had no bathtub. So where was he to bathe? Grandma answered his unasked question. "You bring in that wash tub from the side of the house and then start drawing water for me to heat."

He brought in the tub. "Where shall I put it?" he asked.

"Set it right there beside the stove," Grandma said, "or you'll freeze your hide. These sheets hanging here will give you some privacy." And so it was that Hollis was introduced to the farm ritual of the weekly bath.

The next day was Sunday. After morning chores and breakfast Grandma made a strange announcement. "Today's Methodist Sunday, so we'll worship at home." To Hollis' questioning look she answered, "We Baptists share the church building with the Methodists. One week the Baptist pastor preaches, the next week it's the Methodist pastor. We usually worship at home on Methodist Sundays, because their services just don't feel right. Now go upstairs and get cleaned up. Put on your good shirt."

"Who else is coming?" he asked, hoping she would say Gibby was coming.

"It's just us," she replied.

Hollis protested, "But Grandma, why do I have to wear a clean shirt if no one will see it?"

"The Lord will see it. Now scoot," she replied.

Hollis did as he was told, and when he returned downstairs he found Grandma and Grandpa already seated at the table. A fresh linen tablecloth had been laid, and two candles burned in the center of the table. The big family Bible lay open before Grandpa. Grandpa had his hair slicked down and was wearing a clean white shirt with a starched collar. Grandma was wearing a dress Hollis had not seen before, and a prim hat decorated with dried strawflowers was perched on her head.

As soon as Hollis was seated, Grandpa began reading from the Bible the story about the prodigal son. It told about a farmer who had two sons, one who worked hard on the farm and one who went away and wasted all his time and money. When the wasteful son finally returned home, the father was so glad to see him that he forgot to be angry with him for being so foolish. Instead he held a feast to celebrate his homecoming. Grandpa's voice seemed to tremble as he read.

When the story was finished Grandma said a prayer, saying how thankful they were that Hollis had been sent to live with them. Hollis had never heard his name mentioned in a prayer before, and it made him feel a little embarrassed, but glad at the same time. As soon as the prayer was over, Grandma blew out the candles and everyone went to change back into their everyday clothes.

Because it was Sunday, only the basic daily chores were done—feeding the stock, cleaning out their pens, milking the cows, gathering the eggs and bringing in water and firewood. Hollis decided to use the free time to explore the farm.

First he went to the pond and began working his way around its edge. He came to its outlet, where the creek continued on its way past the barns and across the meadow. He made his way across the creek by hopping from stone to stone, and then balancing on a partially submerged log. Once safe on the other side he congratulated himself that he had managed to stay dry.

He set off to explore the wooded slope on the other side of the pond. As he began to walk up the hill he noticed that the trees here were well spaced, and he could walk among them without having to push his way through a lot of brush. It was the way he had always imagined a park would be. Under his feet a carpet of maple leaves rustled with each step and the sweet smell of autumn greeted his nostrils. He noticed two slight impressions in the earth, apparently made by wagon wheels. The tracks headed diagonally back down the slope, off to his left, and he followed them. As he neared the bottom of the hill, he glimpsed a building nestled in the trees. It was unpainted, and the natural hues of the weather-grayed vertical boards blended so well with the surroundings that he might have missed it entirely had it not been for a ray of sunlight reflecting off the metal roof. In the center of the roof was a long raised section of roof with openings under it. Hollis peered into the spacious windows that lined the south side.

He could not resist the urge to investigate this building. There was no lock on the door, so he raised the latch and went in. After his eyes became adjusted to the dim light of the interior he began to poke around. Lanterns hung from the rafters, but today sunlight streamed in through the windows. In the center of the building was a big open stone structure with metal grates across the top. It was rectangular in shape, with an iron door at one end, and, at the other end, a large stovepipe that extended up through the special two-part roof. Could it have been some kind of fireplace? The opening above it could be to let out the smoke. Off to one side were big iron kettles, similar to the Websters' pig-scalding kettle, an assortment of smaller enamel pots and a small kitchen stove. A cot had been built in one corner of the building, and at the other end was a stack of big crates. Hollis looked inside one of the crates and discovered that it was full of identical tall rectangular cans with handles on top. He pulled one out, realizing from its lightness that it was empty. Next to the crates he found a pasteboard box. It was partially opened, and he couldn't help opening it the rest of the way to peek at its contents. There he found a large stack of what appeared to be paper labels. His eyes widened as he read what was printed on them: "Ingraham & Ingraham, Thurman, New York, Pure Maple Syrup." This was the sugarhouse! His father and Grandpa had built it just like they planned! Sanford Ingraham and Johnny Ingraham. And all of the cans were empty.

Hollis carefully replaced the can in the crate, closed up the labels and studied the sugarhouse more carefully. On the back wall hung a large galvanized washtub. Along the wall were rows and rows of stacks of overturned buckets. A few were made of wood, and the rest were metal. Beside the overturned buckets several buckets had been left upright, all full of cloth sacks of metal tube-like things. In one corner stood wooden boxes of metal lids for the buckets. A large barrel stood in another corner. Two pairs of snow-shoes hung from nails driven into the wood beside the door, their rawhide webbing making a lacy design against the tan of the boards.

Everything was neat and orderly, as though the Ingrahams had walked out and left it yesterday, planning to return today. Hollis went out, making sure the door was latched securely. He circled the building, and discovered a large vat close to the back wall of the sugarhouse. Another large wooden vat was stored behind a wood-shed, which was off to one side of the sugarhouse, but detached from it. The shed was stacked to the rafters with firewood, just waiting to be used. This was a wonderful place, and Hollis stayed for a while, trying to imagine his father and grandfather working there together. Finally his stomach told him it must be near supper-time, so he turned his steps around the pond toward home.

That night, alone in his room, he again picked up the letter he had begun to his mother. He reviewed the events of the day, trying to figure out what he should tell Ma. *This morning at breakfast I mentioned maple syrup and suddenly everyone acted strange. I learned all about Pa and Grandpa and their maple syrup dream.* No, he couldn't mention that; Ma must have known about it, and if she didn't tell him about it, there must be a reason. He picked up his pencil and began to write. "Sunday. Yesterday was washday, and it rained in the afternoon, so we had to bring the clothes inside to dry. I dropped them all on the porch, but Grandma just laughed." He paused, reading it over. Ma would like that, thinking of the laughter. He continued. "Today we had church at home because Grandma said it was 'Methodist Sunday' at the real church. I wonder if she knows that we are Methodists." He thought for a minute and then rubbed out the last sentence. Ma might think there was a problem. Instead he wrote, "Grandpa read the story of the prodigal son and Grandma thanked God for letting me come stay here." He was itching to tell Ma about discovering the sugarhouse, but it might upset her. Ma had enough on her mind. He set the letter down and blew out the lamp, suddenly exhausted. He gave one last look at Crane Mountain. The early evening moonlight faintly showed the outline of the hill across the pond, the hill where the sugarhouse was nestled amongst the trees. He could picture it in his mind's eye, and it comforted him.

6

School

It was dark the next morning when Hollis heard the now-familiar broomstick-rapping on the kitchen ceiling beneath his bed.

"Time to get up and do chores, boy, or you'll be late for school!"

School! Hollis had almost forgotten that today he was to begin classes at the little District Three schoolhouse. He frowned anxiously as he pulled on his barn clothes and splashed his face with water. He didn't mind school itself, but the thought of being thrown in with a new bunch of children was worrisome. One of those children was bound to be Tommy Webster.

He raced downstairs, pulled on his coat, grabbed the slop pail in one hand and the egg basket in the other and raced out to catch up with Grandpa, who was already halfway out to the barn. He emptied the slop pail into the pig trough and watched with amusement for a moment while Maggie snuffled through the potato peels, apple parings and grain that was her breakfast.

"You don't have all day, boy," came Grandpa's sharp reminder.

Hollis launched into the now-familiar routine. He scrambled up the splintery ladder to the loft, picked up a pitchfork and tossed heaping forkfuls of sweet-smelling hay to the barn floor below. He climbed back down, and, while Grandpa began milking Jessie, Hollis loaded the mangers with hay and added the usual scoops of grain. There was some for Jessie, lots for Gwen and Jackie, and a generous share for the sheep. He took the egg basket into the hen house and began collecting the eggs, reaching carefully under each hen in the nesting boxes, and, with his voice as soft as their silky breast feathers, he calmed their anxious clucking and carefully deposited the warm prizes in his basket.

When they returned to the house, Grandma had breakfast on the table, and Hollis rushed to sit down. She caught him as he started to seat himself. "Wait just a minute young man! You go wash the barn smell off you and change out of those clothes before you sit down," she scolded. "And mind you use soap. You won't make any friends smelling like a barn yard."

Hollis went back outside, pumped himself a basin of water and obediently scrubbed his face, neck, hands and forearms with the cold water and strong lye soap. When he was sure he would pass muster, he toweled off, went back inside and ran upstairs to put on his school clothes.

Grandma nodded her approval when he reappeared for breakfast. While he ate his bacon and biscuits, Grandma instructed him on how to proceed. "Go on out to the end of the lane, and like as not you'll meet up with the Centerbar children. You'll know 'em right off because they all have coal-black hair and coal-black eyes. And there's six of them. No seven. No six, I believe. You can walk with them so you have company."

Grandpa snorted. "Some company! They probably won't even talk to you. Them Centerbars are a strange lot, always keeping to themselves."

"Why, of course they'll talk to him. Children are children, no matter."

As Hollis said goodbye, grabbed his dinner pail and headed out the door, he fervently hoped Grandma was right. When he got to the end of the lane, sure enough, scampering down the hill came a troupe of black-haired, black-eyed children chattering among themselves. When they caught sight of Hollis they immediately fell silent and walked with heads bent down and eyes lowered. Hollis fell into step beside them and walked along in silence, studying the strange little group. Like the Websters, the Centerbar children came in all sizes, from a boy who was slightly taller than Hollis down to a little boy who couldn't have been more than six years old. All of them were thin and dressed in ill-fitting hand-me-down clothes, with homemade shoes of rawhide. There were four girls and two boys, and Hollis noted that when they thought he wasn't looking, they all peeked at him from beneath their thick black lashes. He was just trying to think of something to say to break the silence, when the youngest tripped on a rut in the road and lurched forward. Instinctively Hollis lunged to grab him and just managed to scoop him up by his armpits before his face could scrape the gravelly road.

"Here you go," Hollis said, setting him gently back onto his feet.

The boy stared at him with his wide dark eyes. "Thank you!" he gulped.

"Yeah, thanks," chimed in the older boy. Then he added awkwardly, "My name is Nicholas."

"Mine's Hollis," he responded.

"These are my sisters, Jacqueline, Marie, Anne and Thérèse," he said, nodding at each of them in turn, "and this," he said picking up his brother, "is Jean-Paul. Here, Jean-Paul, you can ride piggy-back for awhile."

They started off toward school again, and slowly, haltingly, they began to make conversation. The Centerbar children were very impressed to learn that Hollis had lived in Warrensburg, a town they had never seen, and asked him many questions about life in town. Were there fancy hotels? And big stores? And did the ladies there wear feathered hats and dresses made of silk? Was it true that there were factories bigger than ten churches put together? Had he ever seen a train? Hollis answered all their questions, feeling pangs of homesickness as he described the wide tree-lined streets of Warrensburg crowded with clattering wagons and buggies. He told of the mill district along River Street and of the tannery and described the pungent aroma that still emanated from the remaining hemlock bark piles. He didn't mention that other smell, the smell of death.

With words he painted a picture of the churches, stores, hotels, blacksmith shops and livery stables. He realized suddenly that it might sound like bragging, so he stopped his description and abruptly said, "Well, that's what Warrensburg's like. It's different from here. But here you have nice farms and lots of animals. And you have this beautiful mountain," he added, pointing toward Crane Mountain, now behind them.

The children all looked where he pointed, as if seeing Crane for the first time. "No mountain?" asked Marie in disbelief.

"Nope, not like that one," Hollis said.

The rest of the walk to school was filled with chatter from the younger children about how glorious it must be to live in a big town. "Is everybody rich there?" Thérèse wanted to know.

Hollis thought of the shabby home he and Ma had shared, and the constant struggle to survive. He laughed in spite of himself. "No," he said kindly, "not everybody."

All too soon they arrived at the little white clapboard schoolhouse at the Kenyontown corners. Several other children who had arrived early were engaged in an energetic game of tag in the schoolyard. No one made a move to include Hollis and the Centerbars, so they just stood by and watched until the loud ringing of the school bell cut the game short.

The schoolteacher stood in the doorway, and Hollis caught his breath in surprise. Unlike the stern-faced elderly spinster who had been his teacher in Warrensburg, this woman was young and pretty. Her auburn hair was drawn back from her smooth ivory face and hung in curls at her neck. She wore a crisp white blouse and a skirt the color of her sapphire-blue eyes. A matching shawl was pulled around her shoulders.

"Good morning, Seth. Good morning, Elizabeth. What a pretty frock, Marie!" she said, greeting each child warmly as the students entered the building. When it was Hollis' turn she said, "And you must be Hollis Ingraham!" She seemed not to notice that Hollis was blushing as he nodded his response. "Your grandmother told me that you'd be joining us. My name is Miss Kenyon. Just hang your coat on a hook and take a seat over there on that second bench on the right.

Hollis looked around. Just inside the door were rows of hooks on which to hang coats. Before him he could see one large classroom. A big box stove was centered on the near end of the room,

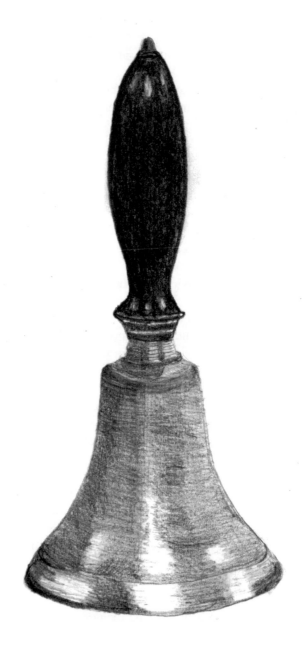

Miss Kenyon's Bell

with its stovepipe running the length of the room into a chimney that shared the opposite wall with a large slate. In front of the slate stood an oak table that he assumed was the teacher's desk. Along each side of the room ran two rows of low benches, each with one long desk stretching in front of it. Hollis followed the example of the other children and stashed his coat and dinner pail by the door before going to sit on the bench Miss Kenyon had pointed out. Nicholas sat beside him.

The room filled with chattering children, and most of them were staring openly at Hollis. Miss Kenyon closed the door and moved to the front of the room. All talking ceased, and the students scurried to their seats and turned their attention to her. "Good morning, boys and girls!" she said.

"Good morning, Miss Kenyon," returned a chorus of twenty-two voices.

"This morning we have–" she began, but was interrupted when the schoolhouse door burst open and the Webster children straggled in.

A note of reproach entered Miss Kenyon's voice as she said, "Good morning, Tom, Charlotte. Good morning, Clarence. Lulu, Lila, good morning. Please take your seats right away. I've asked you to try harder to be on time."

Hollis was secretly pleased to see Tom Webster being scolded by the beautiful Miss Kenyon. They quickly took their seats, Tommy sitting on the other side of Nicholas, the only seat left.

Miss Kenyon began again, "This morning we are happy to welcome a new student, Hollis Ingraham. Say 'Welcome, Hollis.'"

Again the students chorused, saying, "Welcome, Hollis!" But Hollis could hear Tommy Webster's voice standing out slightly from the other voices, just loud enough for him to hear, "Welcome, Pukey!"

Hollis felt his face redden, and he dropped his eyes, pretending to examine the desktop. What happened next confused him. Tommy Webster suddenly yelped. When Hollis looked over he could see no cause for it. Nicholas was sitting with his hands innocently folded on the desk, seeming not to notice Tommy's glare.

"Gentlemen! What's going on back there?" Miss Kenyon demanded sternly.

"Nothin'," Tommy said angrily.

"Nothing, Ma'am," said Nicholas, his face revealing nothing.

"Well, then, let's begin our morning lessons." She began assigning work to each group of children, from the youngest to the oldest, in some cases instructing an older student to help younger ones. Soon the room was humming with students reading aloud to one another, studying maps and working arithmetic problems.

Miss Kenyon called Hollis up to her desk. "Hollis, I have no records from your last school, so I'd like to work with you awhile in order to decide what level to place you in." She opened a reader and pointed out a passage for him to read. He breezed through it, so she gave him a passage from another reader. That paragraph was more challenging, but still he read it with no mistakes.

Miss Kenyon's eyebrows raised in surprise. "Very good!" she exclaimed. "Let's try some arithmetic now." She quickly wrote four problems on the slate. Hollis had no trouble with the first three, but the fourth involved dividing fractions, and it slowed him down a bit.

"Yes, yes. That's right," Miss Kenyon said, smiling. "You've been going to school quite regularly, haven't you?"

"Yes, ma'am."

"You haven't had to miss school in the fall to help with the harvest, or in the spring to help with the sugaring and planting, have you?"

"No, ma'am."

"I wish that were true of all my students," Miss Kenyon said with a sigh. "I'm going to have you work with the oldest students. You may share books with Nicholas."

Hollis returned to his seat and was soon hard at work. Before he knew it, Miss Kenyon announced that it was lunchtime. Out came the dinner pails. Hollis opened his to discover it packed with biscuits spread with fresh butter and gooey jam. There were also slabs of cheese and a fat green pear. He was enjoying the biscuits immensely when he glanced over to see Nicholas pull a little apple from the pocket of his faded shirt and devour all of it except the stem. There was no other food in sight. Hollis knew how hunger must have gnawed at him.

Hollis pushed two of the biscuits toward Nicholas. "Can you eat these?" he asked. "My grandma packed way too much. I'm stuffed."

Nicholas hesitated only a moment before gratefully accepting. Then, to Hollis' surprise, he went to distribute pieces of the biscuits among his sisters and Jean Paul, saving none for himself. Hollis made a mental note to try to bring more food the next day. He gave the cheese to Nicholas and ate the pear.

As the children were finishing their lunches, one of the oldest girls, a red-haired girl, took a pail of fresh cold water around the room, allowing each student to drink a dipperful.

"That's Iva Wainwright," Nicholas told Hollis. "She always gets to bring the water around because she pouts if she doesn't get picked."

Iva overheard him and glared at Nicholas. She flounced away, deliberately passing him by with the dipper.

Hollis looked up in surprise. "You skipped him," he said.

"Centerbars always go last," she said with a disdainful sniff.

"Iva!" The teacher said, plainly annoyed. "I've spoken to all of you children about that! I'll have no more of this behavior. Now— out for recess, and play nicely."

The children burst from the schoolhouse like water gushing over a spillway and then clustered into little groups. On one side of the building younger children were getting up a game of Tillie-over. A group of older girls were clumped together near the lilac bush, whispering and giggling and passing a note around. Tommy Webster was talking secretively with a bunch of the older boys over by the woodshed, and glancing in Hollis' direction.

"Uh-oh, looks like we're in for trouble," said Nicholas, at Hollis' elbow.

"What do you mean?" Hollis asked.

Before he had a chance to wonder any more, he heard a loud burst of laughter from the boys, followed by Tommy Webster saying in a high-pitched voice, "Oh, you've been going to school quite regularly, haven't you, Pukey?"

The boys roared with amusement, and Tommy, encouraged, continued in his falsetto voice, "Oh, Pukey, I wish that all of my students were bur-rill-yant like you!"

With that remark the boys circled Hollis and Nicholas, taunting and jeering loudly, "Pukey, Pukey! Bur-rill-yant town boy can't handle a little pig's blood!"

"Hey, leave him alone!" Nicholas shouted.

"Shut up, half-breed!" Tommy shouted back.

Nobody knew for sure who threw the first punch, but suddenly fists were flying. Hollis felt knuckles graze his cheekbone and swung as hard as he could in retaliation, connecting with Tommy Webster's chin and sending him sprawling on the ground.

The girls standing nearby screamed, and Hollis could hear Iva calling out, "Teacher! Teacher! Fight!" Tommy lunged at Hollis then, grabbing him around the waist and wrestling him to the ground. Out of the corner of his eye Hollis could see Nicholas exchanging blows with one of Tommy's friends.

A stern voice cut through the fracas. "Stop this fighting instantly!"

The hem of a long blue skirt swished past Hollis, and he looked up to see Miss Kenyon angrily surveying the scene. "What is the meaning of this?" she demanded.

The boys stood wordlessly, staring at the ground.

"Tommy," she persisted, "Who started this?"

Tommy shrugged his shoulders.

"Hollis, can you tell me what's going on?"

"No, ma'am," Hollis said, shaking his head.

"Nicholas?"

Nicholas looked questioningly at Hollis, but seeing Hollis' scowl, merely shook his head.

"Leonard?" she asked the fourth boy.

"No, ma'am," he answered.

"Then I have no choice but to keep all four of you after school today. Now, come. It's time to go in for afternoon classes."

The students filed quietly into the classroom and took their seats. The remainder of the day went without incident, and when the rest of the children were dismissed, Hollis, Nicholas, Tommy and Leonard were instructed to write "I will not fight" on the slate one hundred times. When they were done, Miss Kenyon sent Leonard up the road to the Burdick's well to get a pail of water. He and Nicholas had to erase and wash the slate and take the erasers outside to clap the chalk dust out of them. Tommy swept the classroom floor and then swept out the boys' and girls' outhouses behind the school, while Hollis carried in wood and stacked it, ready for the morning fire. This accomplished, Miss Kenyon sat them down. Hollis steeled himself for a lecture, but he was not prepared for what was to come.

Miss Kenyon looked sad rather than angry, and her voice had lost its stern tone. "I want you to know how disappointed I am with your behavior today," she began softly. The boys lowered their heads.

"Nothing is accomplished by violence. We must learn to accept each other's differences and work out problems by discussing them. In the future, this is what I will expect of you. Understand?"

"Yes, Miss Kenyon," they said in unison. Hollis felt so awful, he almost wished she had yelled at him the way his teacher in Warrensburg would have.

"Good. Let's have you shake hands and we'll start fresh tomorrow," she said, walking to the desk to pick up her shawl. "Let's go home."

They left the school and headed out their various ways. Miss Kenyon went north on the Johnsburg Road toward the Pascos' house where she was boarding. Leonard went south, and Tommy, Nicholas and Hollis began trudging down Mill Creek Road, kicking little clods of dirt ahead of them.

7

Friends

It was Tommy who finally broke the silence. "Thanks for not telling on me. She would've sent a note home and Pa would've give me a lickin' for sure."

Hollis said nothing.

Tommy began again. "Look, Hollis, I'm sorry I called you—that name, all right?"

Hollis stopped walking. "It wasn't just me you called a name," he said, nodding toward Nicholas. "What about him?"

"What name?" Tommy asked in surprise. "'Half-breed?' That's not a name, that's what he is! Ask anybody!"

"Well, I think it sounds like a name," Hollis said stubbornly, his chin jutting out.

"Oh, all right. I'm sorry," Tommy said to Nicholas, a bit grudgingly.

Just then they came to a small pond beside the road. "Hey," said Tom, the argument already forgotten, "let's skip rocks across the pond!"

All three boys put down their books and lunch pails and began collecting stones, looking for the smoothest, flattest ones they could find. Tommy, seeing Hollis getting ready to throw, said, "Not here—too many cattails in the way. Let's go around to this side."

He led the way to an open spot on the bank of the pond where they took turns hurling their ammunition, using a sidearm delivery and counting the number of times each stone skipped off the surface before sinking into the murky water. Hollis had saved his flattest stone for last, and now gave it a powerful snap. Tommy counted, "One, two, three, four, five, six, seven, eight, NINE! I can't believe it!" he said admiringly. "That's the best throw I've ever seen! It'll be great to have you play ball with us!" Hollis shrugged off the compliment, but inwardly glowed, feeling much better about his future at this new school.

As the boys turned from the pond and headed back to the road, Hollis' foot dislodged something half-covered with soggy marsh grass. He knew at once that it wasn't a rock; it moved too easily and made a hollow noise when his foot struck it. He bent down and parted the grass to inspect the object. The others stopped to see what had caught his attention.

"Hey," Hollis exclaimed, picking it up, "it's a turtle shell!" He ran his hand over the domed top, his fingers tracing its irregular plates and gently rubbing the worn areas along its decorative borders where the brownish-black had given way to bony white.

Nicholas and Tommy drew near to see what he had found. Nicholas said admiringly, "Say, that's a beauty!"

"What kind of turtle do you think it is?" Hollis asked.

"A dead one!" Tommy snorted, and began to laugh loudly, oblivious to the fact that Hollis and Nicholas showed no appreciation for his humor. Hollis, in fact, seemed somewhat sobered, and stretched his hand away from his body, as if to distance himself from the shell.

Nicholas took it from his hand. "Let me show you something," he said. Moving to the pond's edge, he immersed the shell in the water. The dull, drab brown turned a rich and glossy greenish-brown, with its delicate markings sharply gleaming. "See? It's like it's alive again."

"Hey, fellas, I gotta get home," Tommy interrupted. "You can stay here all day if you want to, but I'll catch it good from my pa if I ain't home quick."

"Go on, then," said Nicholas impatiently.

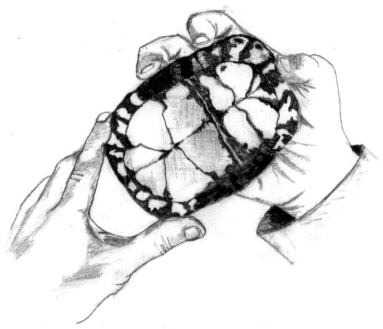

The Shell

Hollis said nothing, not even raising his eyes from the shell. "Do you think that's what it's like?" he asked after Tommy was safely out of earshot.

"What what is like?"

"You know. Being dead. I mean people." He turned the shell over in his hands, absently touching the flat plate that had protected the turtle's belly, but really studying its emptiness. "Do you think you die and then you just aren't there anymore?"

Nicholas spoke slowly. "I don't know anyone who's dead, except the Pascos' little baby, and I didn't really know him. Do you know someone who's dead?"

Hollis nodded. He didn't know if the words would come out. "My father is dead. He died when I was little." Suddenly the story he thought he couldn't begin became a tale he couldn't stop. "I was little, but I remember the day it happened. Two men came to our house and they were talking in low voices to my mother, something about a fire—a fire at a tannery! That's it, at a tannery! They said my pa was lost. That's the word they used, 'lost.' My ma cried out and almost fell down. They had to help her to a chair. She kept saying over and over again, 'Not my Johnny! Not my Johnny! He wasn't even supposed to be there!' When I went over to see what was wrong, she grabbed me and started crying. I asked her why they couldn't find my pa, and she just kept crying and saying how he wasn't supposed to be there. It scared me. Then I don't remember too much. There were a lot of people around, talking and crying, and a funeral. Then we moved away, and my mother never really talked about my father again. After we moved, I never saw my grandparents again until now."

"Never? How come?"

Hollis shrugged. "I don't know. Ma never told me. I think there was some kind of fight, about my father or money or something."

Nicholas shook his head. "Grown-ups do strange things." He handed Hollis the shell as they turned homeward. "You should keep this for good luck. My mother says her people believe turtles are a good sign."

"Your mother's people?" Hollis asked.

"My mother is a full-blooded Abenaki Indian. That's why Tom called me a half-breed. Everyone does. I don't care. The Abenaki are a proud people, with a long history of courage and honor. It doesn't really matter what anybody calls you; it just matters that you know who you are."

"What do you mean?" Hollis asked.

"Well," Nicholas said, "It's like my name. Everyone calls us 'Centerbar,' but that's not really our name. My papa is French, from Canada, and his name is Jacques St. Hubert." Nicholas pronounced it "Zhak Sant Eeyew-bare." He continued, "People here had trouble pronouncing the French. They thought it sounded like 'Jock Centerbar,' so that's what they called him. It doesn't matter; we are who we are. And I am proud of who I am. See?"

Hollis shook his head. "I don't know. I guess so."

Nicholas stopped and turned to face Hollis. "We are proud to be named for St. Hubert. Do you know his story?"

Hollis shook his head. He had never heard of St. Hubert.

"I'll tell you what Mama and Papa told me. Many centuries ago, there was an important young man who was an attendant in the court of the King of France. He had been married, but his wife died. One day, on Good Friday, he was out hunting—he loved to hunt— and he saw a huge buck. Instead of running away, this buck turned and faced him, holding its head up high. It was unlike any other deer the young man had ever seen, for between its antlers stood a shining cross."

"A real cross? Like in church?" Hollis wanted to know.

Nicholas nodded and continued, "The young man, who was not a Christian, heard a voice telling him he must change his life. He gave up all his great wealth and devoted his life to serving God. He became a Bishop, and later was named a saint. Today St. Hubert is known as the patron saint of hunters." They stopped then at the turnoff to the Ingraham farm. "So," Nicholas concluded, "We are proud to bear the name of St. Hubert, and it doesn't matter if people call us 'Centerbar,' or 'half-breed', for that matter, because we know where we come from. And the way we act every day to honor our past makes us who we are. Get it?"

This time Hollis nodded. It made more sense now. "You mean, if you act in a way that would make your ancestors proud of you, you can be proud of yourself no matter what anyone calls you?" he asked.

"That's exactly what I mean. Here's where I leave you. See you tomorrow!" Nicholas continued up French Hill, while Hollis turned down the road to the farm and broke into a trot, trying to find words to explain to his grandparents his reason for being so late.

Grandpa was just returning from the barn when Hollis reached the house. "You're late," he said.

"Yes, sir."

"Well get inside. Barn chores are all done, but your grandma's got work waiting."

Grandma was standing at the stove when they entered the kitchen. Wiping her hands on her apron, she approached them. "How was your first day of school? You're mighty late getting home." She stopped suddenly, catching sight of Hollis' face. "What's this? Come on over here by the lamp. Why, you've got a scrape on your cheek, and a shiner, too, if I don't miss my guess. Have you been fighting, boy?"

Hollis nodded.

"Did you start it?"

"No, ma'am."

"Did you give as good as you got?"

"I think so."

"Who was it with?"

"Tommy Webster."

"Ah," Grandma said knowingly. "This wouldn't have had anything to do with the pig slaughtering?"

"Yes."

"Ah-ha. Well, now that's over and done with. Tom Webster's not a bad boy. He'll let it go now. You let it go, too. Understand?"

Hollis nodded.

"Good. Now get the wood box filled, carry in some water and wash up for supper."

After dinner Hollis did his lessons at the dining table while Grandma worked on the ironing and asked him about school. Grandpa, silent as usual, busied himself with cleaning and oiling tools to keep the wooden handles from rotting and the metal parts from rusting.

Hollis, feeling his eyelids drooping, said goodnight to his grandparents and hiked up the steep steps to his room. It had been a long day and he ached for sleep, but he knew he should write something in his letter to Ma. He turned up his lantern and carefully wrote, "Monday. Today was my first day of school. Tommy Webster and I..." he paused and thought ...*got into a fight because he made a fool of me in front of everyone and called my friend a half-breed.* No, he couldn't worry Ma with stories about fights, even if he wanted to be truthful. Instead he finished, "helped clean up after school with two other boys named Leonard and Nicholas. Nicholas and I read in the highest group" (Ma would like that) "and his last name came from the name of a saint. Do Methodists believe in saints? We found a nice turtle shell by a pond." Should he add that it made him think about Pa, and how he was dead? And how he wanted to know about that?

Just then Grandma gave a little knock at his door and poked her head in. "I finished the ironing. Here are your shirt and trousers." She turned toward the dresser and spotted the turtle shell where he had placed it beside the photograph. "Say, that's a nice shell!" she said admiringly. "Mind if I pick it up?"

Hollis shook his head.

She tapped the shell with her fingernail. "It's good and hard. Not that it did the turtle much good," she added.

"What do you mean?" Hollis asked.

"Well, look—the turtle dragged around all this armor, and something got to him anyway."

"What do you think happened to him?"

"It's hard to say. Something must have gotten at him in spite of the shell." Grandma paused and thought a moment. "It happens to people, too."

Hollis was confused. "To people?" he asked.

"Some people wear shells, too. Oh, not shells like you can see, but a kind of toughness that keeps you away from them, you know?"

Hollis thought of Grandpa and how crusty he was all the time, and nodded.

"Sometimes they think that if they cover up their soft insides they won't get hurt. And sometimes other people wear shells for other reasons. Sometimes they try to cover up when they are sad or scared, so other people won't worry about them."

Without meaning to, Hollis slid his hand over his letter to Ma. "Is that bad?" he asked.

"Not bad, not good. But you can't let the shell be all there is to you. The softness of the turtle was just as important as the shell was, don't you think?"

Hollis nodded.

"That's the part that swam, and climbed out onto a log on a fair day to soak up sunshine, the part that nibbled grass and played with other turtles. That's the part that had a heart and was alive."

Hollis couldn't help himself. "But that's the part that's dead, too."

Grandma sighed. "Yes," she said, "it is. Illness and pain and death come to all of us sooner or later, shell or no shell. That's the plain truth, and it hurts, shell or no shell. So what's the sense of keeping the shell between us and the ones that love us?"

She didn't seem to expect an answer, and Hollis sure didn't have one, so he said nothing. She carefully replaced the shell on the dresser, and her eye fell on the photograph. As if by habit, she picked it up and polished it lovingly with a corner of her apron before setting it down again. "Your father never wore a shell. He had a good heart, and he always let it lead him where it would. He loved life and he loved people. The Lord took him early, but every day of his short life was full and rich with love. If only you could have known him longer!" Grandma sighed again, and then said, "Blow your lamp out soon. Tomorrow's another day. Goodnight now."

"Goodnight, Grandma," Hollis said, setting aside the letter. His grandmother turned to go. "Grandma?" She looked back. "Thanks," he said. After he blew out his lantern, he rolled over onto his side and gave one last look at Crane Mountain. There was something solid and good in the sight, and he snuggled contentedly into his cornhusk mattress, realizing with surprise that he was almost happy here, happy with his grandma, with his new friend Nicholas, and with his new teacher. He even liked his farm chores in a funny kind of way.

Just as he began to doze off, a guilty thought jabbed him. What about Ma? Was everything all right with her? And would she let him know if it weren't? Sleep swallowed him up, guilt and all, and he dreamed he was lying in golden sunshine, feeling its warmth. Ma was with him, and they were stretched out on a log on the side of a pond. He tried to roll over to look at Ma and felt something bulky in his way. He looked down and discovered he was wearing a big, bulky turtle shell. He looked over at Ma, and she was wearing one, too. She looked funny and he began to laugh. Ma just smiled, slipped off the log into the pond and began to swim away. *But I never knew Ma could swim*, he thought in his dream.

8

Gold!

Hollis' first week in Thurman flew by, stuffed with chores, schoolwork, finishing up his first letter to Ma and exploring the farm. Before he knew it, Sunday had arrived again. This time it was Baptist Sunday, and that meant a trip to Kenyontown in the wagon. After chores and breakfast Grandma turned to Grandpa and asked, "Will you be going to church with us today?"

Grandpa shook his head. "I've told you a hundred times, Hazel. I don't have to sit in a pew in a church to talk to the Lord. He can hear me here as good as anywhere."

Grandma shook her head. "Sanford Ingraham, it couldn't have been the Lord who made you this stubborn! At least hitch up the team for us, and we'll say a prayer for you." To Hollis she said, "Scoot, boy, and get ready or we'll be late!"

Hollis ran to change and returned promptly for Grandma's critical inspection. After she slicked down his hair, she pronounced him fit. Grandpa brought the wagon around, and Grandma and Hollis set off for Kenyontown. They rode along in silence for a while, enjoying the crisp autumn day. After a bit Grandma asked, "Do you know how to handle a team?"

When Hollis told her that he'd never tried driving a wagon before, Grandma handed him the reins and showed him how to thread the lines between his fingers and how to guide the horses. "A

70

boy should know his way around horses," she said, "and Gwen and Jackie are as steady a team as you could find to learn on."

She was a patient teacher, and Hollis enjoyed the feeling of power as the team responded to his direction. Before he knew it, they had arrived at the Kenyontown corners. "Haw!" he called out to them, as he reined them left. In just a few minutes they had pulled up in the yard in front of the church and climbed down. Grandma had him lift a heavy flat weight out of the wagon—she called it a "flat iron"—and place it on the ground in front of the horses. Together they looped the reins through the protruding handle to anchor the team while they were at church.

They slipped into one of the dark wooden pews just as the service began. A very plump rosy-cheeked lady began pumping a wheezy organ, and the congregation members rose to their feet and began singing a hymn that Hollis had never heard before. He took the opportunity to look around at his fellow churchgoers. There were the Websters. They took up an entire pew, with Mr. and Mrs. Webster stationed like bookends on the left and right, and all of the children lined up between them. Hollis' eyes wandered up and down the rows of the little church, taking in the older couples, the young families, those well-dressed and those whose worn clothing bespoke hard times. He craned his neck to see those standing on the other side of the big woodstove that heated the building. Suddenly he caught a glimpse of a familiar bushy red beard and he smiled with pleasure as he realized it belonged to Gibby Goodnow, who looked like an over-stuffed sausage in his church outfit.

When the hymn ended and the congregation was seated, Hollis lost his view of Gibby, and he tried to pay attention to the pastor as he announced the day's scripture reading, the one hundred and twenty-first psalm. Grandma quickly flipped open her dog-eared Bible to the appropriate page so she could follow along. The pastor took a deep breath and began to read. "'I will lift up mine eyes unto the hills. From thence cometh my help.'" He continued, but the rest of his words were lost to Hollis, who was already deep in thought. Hollis pictured the grand slopes of Crane Mountain, and the words echoed in his mind, "'From thence cometh my help.'" Was there help there for him? And for Ma? He had to find some way to earn some money, to keep his promise to help Ma. Money. There was no shortage of work on the farm, but it was clear that earning money at it was out of the question. He looked around again at the parishioners around him, now bowing their heads in prayer. Hollis quickly ducked his chin, but continued to size up the situation. Were any of these people well-off enough to pay a hard-working boy a small wage for doing odd jobs? His eye was caught by a nicely dressed older couple near the front of the church. He must find out who they were.

As the minister launched into a lengthy sermon, Hollis' mind danced into fantasy. He imagined himself racing through his daily chores for Grandma and Grandpa, then rushing off to work for the elderly couple. They would marvel at how quickly and neatly he stacked wood, how he carried water without spilling a drop, how he fed and curried their thoroughbreds and polished their fine buggy (surely this couple would have a fine buggy!) to a fare-thee-well. "What a good worker!" they would exclaim. "Here's your pay, and here's a little something extra for working so quickly." Hollis could hear the clink of the gold coins as they dropped into his hand.

A sharp jab from Grandma's elbow interrupted his reverie, and he sheepishly took the collection plate she handed him and passed it on down the pew.

When church was over there was a general exchange of pleasantries among the townsfolk. Many made a point of singling out Grandma and Hollis for special attention, saying such things as, "Why, Hazel, it's good to see you this morning. And who do we have here?" or "This isn't your Johnny's boy, so grown up already!" or "So this is young Hollis! I think he favors the Ingraham side, doesn't he?"

Hollis smiled politely until his face ached, feeling like an exhibit at the fair. It was Gibby who finally came to the rescue, strolling over and clapping him on the shoulder with his giant hand. "Here's my partner! How's it going?"

Hollis grinned with relief and answered, "Fine!"

"I came to ask your Grandma if she can spare you to go hunting next Saturday."

"That would be nice," Grandma replied. "Would you like to go along?" she asked Hollis.

"I don't know how to hunt," he answered disappointedly, "and anyway, I don't have a gun."

"You don't need a gun. You can help drive the deer if you've a mind to come," Gibby reassured him.

"I'd like that."

"Good, then. It's settled. I'll pick you up early in the forenoon, and we'll make a hunter out of you," Gibby said, boosting him up onto the wagon seat and helping Mrs. Ingraham up. He handed Hollis the flat iron to stow under the wagon seat, took the halter of the near horse and maneuvered them out of the crowded yard of the church, nodding approvingly as Hollis took up the reins and clucked to the team.

The next morning Hollis bounded out of bed before Grandpa had a chance to bang on the ceiling. The house was cold, and he leaped into his clothes in record time. He padded down to the kitchen in his stockinged feet, lit the lamp and poked up the coals in the stove. He added some small sticks and blew on the fire to get it going, and then pulled on his coat and boots. Lighting the lantern that hung by the door, he adjusted the flame and carried it out into the cold morning to do his chores. After throwing down the hay and graining the livestock, he cleaned out the pens and gathered the eggs. Grandpa would do the milking when he got down.

It was just getting light when Hollis went back to the house to pump a pail of water for Grandma, clean up and have breakfast. Now that he had proved he could do his chores quickly, he would ask Grandma and Grandpa if he could look for outside work. If they agreed, he would start making inquiries at the store and at larger homes after school.

At least, that was his plan.

He asked them at breakfast. To his surprise, after exchanging glances, his grandparents agreed to his plan. "It's all the same to me," Grandpa said.

"And as long as you get your chores done and your lessons don't suffer," Grandma added.

Hollis gulped the last of his breakfast and set out for school. Arriving at the end of the lane early, he decided to explore the bank of the stream while he waited for Nicholas and the other Centerbars to come down French Hill. He found a long stick on the ground and began wandering along the bank, poking at rocks and probing under submerged logs with it. Suddenly the sun, filtering through the trees, reflected off of something shiny beneath the surface of the water. Hollis stretched to get a better look, but the swirling water of the fast-moving brook made it impossible to see. Gingerly he reached his leg out to step onto a mossy rock in midstream, and the next thing he knew he was sitting in the icy waters of Glen Creek. For a moment he didn't notice, because right in front of him was the shiny object! Mindless of the cold he plunged his arm into the water and scooped the shiny golden lump from the creek bed.

"Hey, what are you doing?" It was Nicholas, Jean-Paul and the girls.

"Are you crazy?" demanded Jacqueline. "You'll catch your death!"

"Gold!" Hollis exulted. "I've found gold! I'll be rich!"

"Let me see gold!" insisted little Marie.

They all crowded around Hollis as he emerged dripping from the creek, his pants completely drenched and his shirt and jacket soaked from the wrist to above the elbow.

"Gold! It is gold!" said Jean-Paul, jumping up and down.

"I'm not so sure," Nicholas said, studying the rock. "The fact is, I think it's what they call 'fool's gold'. Papa showed me some before."

Hollis' heart plummeted, his dream of wealth now as squelched and cold as he was. He kicked a stone dejectedly. "I thought maybe I could find enough so Ma wouldn't have to work at the hotel anymore."

"Sorry, Hollis," Nicholas said sympathetically. "Too bad it's not gold."

"But there is gold up on the mountain!" piped up Marie, taking his hand comfortingly in her small one.

"Yeah," said Jean-Paul, "there's always the treasure on the mountain!"

Hollis' heart raced anew. "What treasure?"

"Oh," said Nicholas reluctantly, "there's supposed to be some gold buried on Crane Mountain, but nobody knows where."

"In a cave. Everybody knows it's in a cave," said Marie impatiently.

"What are you all talking about?" It was Tommy Webster, who had just run out of his yard to join them.

Hollis wished they could keep it a secret, but Marie was not to be silenced. "Hollis thought he found gold, only it wasn't, so we're telling him about the gold on Crane Mountain."

"It was supposedly left there by a general in the Revolutionary War," contributed Anne.

"It was the French and Indian War, and he was a colonel," Tommy argued.

"He was escaping to Canada, and the army was chasing him. When he thought they were going to catch up with him, he hid it," Thérèse chimed in.

"And he didn't hide it alone. Indians helped him carry it up the mountain and put it in a cave," Jean-Paul volunteered proudly.

"How come no one goes and gets it?" Hollis asked in amazement.

Tommy snorted. "It ain't like no one's tried. It's hid, and nobody can find it."

"I'll find it!" Hollis declared rashly, and at that moment he was certain that he would, for after all, wasn't that what the scripture lesson had promised? It had to be a message for him! "From thence cometh my help." Suddenly it all made sense. He could scarcely think of another thing besides finding the golden treasure.

A lifetime passed before recess arrived and he had a chance to get Nicholas alone and get more details. Nicholas good-naturedly answered all of his questions as well as he could, reminding Hollis that this was just a legend, and probably wasn't true. Outwardly Hollis agreed, but inwardly he was convinced that the gold was there, and that it was just waiting for him to discover it. "Tell me about the mountain anyway," he said.

Obligingly Nicholas told him about the trail up Crane from the top of French Hill, and a second trail up to Crane Mountain Pond, on the west side of the mountain.

"But what about caves?" Hollis wanted to know.

"The only cave I've ever seen lies along the trail to the pond," the older boy said. "You have to crawl into it on your belly. And I know there's no gold in it, because I've looked. Everybody's looked."

"Mm-hmm," Hollis said noncommittally.

All the way home from school that afternoon Hollis barely heard the chatter of the Centerbar and Webster children as they frolicked along the frozen road. He would climb the mountain just as soon as he could round up supplies for the expedition, he decided. He wouldn't tell Grandma and Grandpa, as he suspected they would not approve, and he didn't want to have to openly disobey them. And even if they didn't approve, how could they be angry with him when he came home bearing gold?

Gold! He could just picture it—big bars of gold, gold coins, perhaps even gold jewelry encrusted with gems. It would probably be in some kind of trunk or chest with rusty hinges, secured by a big brass lock.

"Well, did you get one?" Grandma's voice startled him out of his daydreams. She was out on the porch shaking rugs when he arrived home from school.

"Hunh?" he asked dumbly.

"Did you get the job you were after?"

"Oh, I forgot!" Hollis said, feeling foolish. The idea of doing odd jobs for pennies, so attractive this morning, had been jostled aside by grand visions of vast fortune, visions he did not want to share just now.

"Forgot!" Grandma exclaimed. "It certainly amazes me the way the mind of young'un works! Just don't be forgetting your chores. I've got bread and honey when you come in."

Hollis left his dinner pail on the porch and went out to help with chores while it was still light. All the time he worked, he mulled over the best way to tackle the mountain. When Grandpa was ready to return to the house, Hollis made an excuse to linger behind in the barn. Looking around he discovered several items that might prove useful. There was a coil of rope hanging from a peg on one of the columns supporting the barn loft. He stuffed it into a grain sack and added a shovel with a broken handle, just the right size to fit inside.

He spotted a hatchet, and he put that in as well. Seeing nothing else, he tucked the sack under his coat and returned to the house, running up to his room to hide it.

Later that night, at supper, Hollis realized he would need some light in order to see inside the cave. While Grandma was busy with the supper dishes he tied up in a handkerchief a handful of the burned-down candle stubs that were saved for starting fires. He added them, along with a dozen wooden matches, to the pack hidden under his bed.

When Hollis blew out his lantern that night, he rolled over once more to look at the mountain. The moon was not quite so bright this night, but the mountain was clearly visible, standing staunchly by like an old friend. "Tomorrow," he thought, closing his eyes, "I'll be there."

When he opened his eyes again it was pitch black, but the chiming of the clock on the kitchen shelf announced that it was five o'clock.

He crept from under cozy bedclothes into the brutally cold morning air and reached under his bed for his bag of supplies. He must get this out of the house and hidden behind the large maple tree down the lane before Grandma and Grandpa awoke. He would retrieve it later, when he headed off toward school. Of course, he wouldn't actually be going to school today, he thought, considering for the first time what Miss Kenyon would think when she found out he had played hooky. She would be disappointed in him at first, but he was sure she would understand when she found out about the gold. Maybe he could give her one of the pieces of jewelry, a nice brooch, perhaps. Maybe there would be two nice pins, and he could give one to Grandma, too. And maybe there would be something in there that would make even the Sour Man happy.

Hollis shook his head impatiently. First things first. Taking the sack, he sneaked barefoot along the hall and down the stairs, noiselessly raising and lowering the latch on the stairway door. He eased himself across the kitchen and through the front door without so much as a creak. After squeezing the door shut behind him, he felt his way to the edge of the porch and stepped off. He was totally unprepared for the surprise that awaited him. With no warning he plunged his bare foot into knee-deep snow. Snow! This ruined everything! It would make the trails difficult or impossible to navigate, and might even obscure the opening to the cave. As much as he hated to, he would have to delay his trip.

With great disappointment he hoisted the bag of supplies and went back into the kitchen, accidentally bumping into a chair.

"That you, boy?" called Grandpa in a raspy voice.

"Just stoking the fire!" Hollis lied, hiding the bag inside the stairway and rattling the grate on the stove.

"That's a good boy," Grandma said.

Feeling ashamed, Hollis added some kindling and small sticks to the fire and opened the draft. The fire began to draw and the kindling burst into flames. Hollis lit the kitchen lamp and returned to his room with the bag. He crammed the bag back under his bed and draped an old shirt over it.

Shivering uncontrollably, he crawled back under his covers to try to warm himself and reorganize his thoughts. This was the first snow they had had, save a few flurries. Surely it could not amount to much, and would disappear as quickly as it had come. He would simply wait until then. The gold wouldn't be going anywhere. Snow was still falling heavily when Hollis finished chores and waded back to the house. His trousers were wet to above his knees, and snow coated his clothing, hair and eyelashes.

Grandma peered out the window, sizing up the dull gray sky. "Looks like it means to keep this up all day. I guess you could get to school, but no telling if you could get back again, so I'll be keeping you home today."

Hollis nodded. He would miss going to school, for he wanted to talk to Nicholas about his plan, but it had been difficult going just from the barn to the house. Walking the two miles to and from school would be too difficult today. The Centerbars might be staying home, too.

As it was, work took up a good part of the morning, for Hollis had to shovel a path to the barn. Then he had to shovel another path down to the creek so the stock could get to water.

They spent the rest of the morning near the fire, which crackled cheerfully. Grandpa settled into his favorite chair with his pipe, his bad leg stretched toward the fire, maintaining and repairing his hand tools. Hollis watched him whet the blades of sickles and scythes, brush rust from iron, repair split handles and smooth away splinters. Each tool was lovingly rubbed with oil until it gleamed in the lamplight.

Grandma was busily knitting with her butternut-dyed wool. "Come, let me see your hand," she commanded Hollis. Obediently he stretched his hand toward her. "Not like that!" she laughed. "Make a fist."

He did as told and she measured the distance around his fist with a scrap of yarn. "There! Now I know how long to make your socks. If you're going hunting with Gibby Saturday you'll be needing some good warm ones."

He had almost forgotten about Gibby's invitation. "Do you suppose they'll still go? With the snow and all?"

"Snow makes the tracking easier. They'll go if it's not too deep," Grandpa said.

"I hope the snow won't be too deep," Hollis said.

9

The Deer Hunt

By Saturday some of the snow had melted and the rest had settled to a compact six-inch layer, not too much for a hunting trip. Hollis was up at five, hurrying to get his work done before Gibby arrived to pick him up. He finished up with the animals and proceeded to haul in buckets of water to be heated for washday.

Grandma had outfitted Hollis with some extra-warm clothes. He had on his union suit, a wool shirt of Grandpa's with the sleeves turned up, heavy trousers and the thick new socks Grandma had just finished the night before. He could barely squeeze his feet into his boots with the added thickness of the socks. When he heard Gibby's big feet stomping off snow out on the porch, he hurried to get his coat, a scarf, and some old mittens Grandma found for him.

"Tell Gibby to come in for a cup of coffee!" Grandma said.

Eager to be off, Hollis inwardly groaned, but went outside and relayed the invitation.

"Thank you kindly, Hazel," Gibby said warmly, coming in, "but the boy and I had better be making tracks. We're supposed to meet the Pasco boys on the ridge, and I'd hate to keep them waiting in this cold."

"Then I'll keep the pot hot for when you come back," she said. "Good luck in the hunt."

They left the house before daylight, and Gibby struck off toward the pond. Hollis was surprised, and said, "You know about the shortcut?"

"Sure," Gibby said. "Your Pa and I used it for years, traipsing back and forth. We used to have a good path beaten down. And now you've discovered it, too."

Hollis hesitated a moment, and then decided to entrust Gibby with his secret. "I come over here all the time. I like to go visit the sugarhouse whenever I can."

"Your Grandpa know you go over there?" Gibby asked, his eyebrows raised.

"I haven't told him I found it. I thought he might be mad. I mean, I don't do anything bad there or anything. I just like to go there to sit and think."

Gibby nodded. "They had such dreams for that place, your pa and grandpa. It was like part of them was built into it."

"I know. Grandma told me. But Grandpa never made syrup after my pa died?"

"Not a drop. I offered to help him, but he said he had no heart for it. It's a real shame. He has a fine sugarhouse. Ingraham syrup was the best syrup around, but the fire that killed Johnny killed all that, too."

"Fire?" Hollis asked. "What fire? What happened?"

Gibby looked up in surprise. "Lord, boy. I know you were little when it happened, but didn't your ma ever tell you about it?"

Hollis shook his head, "I overheard some stuff, and I wondered, but I never asked, because I didn't want to upset her. It seemed better not to."

Gibby stroked his beard. "Well, maybe it's not my place to tell you about it, but it's been years, and it seems like you have a right to know. It was the year after he and Sanford finished building the sugarhouse. They were going to make their operation bigger–tap more trees, boil more sap, make more syrup. That meant buying more buckets and taps, and Johnny said they should buy special new 'evaporating pans' like some of the big sugar operations over in Vermont had started using. That way they could make even better syrup—syrup with a lighter color and more delicate flavor. Trouble was, the pans were the latest thing, and they cost a lot of money. Sanford said no, it wasn't worth it, they should just boil the sap down in iron kettles, the old-fashioned way. Johnny, he saw it differently. He was bound and determined to have that new equipment, so he went out and got himself a contract that winter to haul hemlock bark to the tannery in North Creek."

He paused for a moment so they could catch their breath. "That meant he and your Ma had to move up to Johnsburg and rent a place. Sanford was some upset by that, but Johnny thought as soon as he came home with the equipment, everything would be all right."

"What happened?" Hollis asked.

"One day Johnny was delivering a load of bark to the tannery, and a terrible fire broke out in the bark grinding shed. He knew that one of the men who worked at the tannery was trapped inside the shed, and without even thinking, he ran inside to try to get him out. They say the fire got suddenly worse then—almost like an explosion, because of all the dust from the bark—and the whole building went up in flames. Your pa and the other man were lost in the fire. They just never made it out."

"And my grandparents thought it was my ma's fault?" Hollis asked.

"Your ma's fault! Why would they think that?" Gibby asked incredulously.

Hollis was about to tell Gibby about the argument he had overheard his grandparents having, but just then they heard a shout off to their right.

"That's the Pasco boys coming," Gibby said. "They're right on schedule. We should reach the top of the ridge the same time they do. Gibby gestured toward the top of the hill that lay at the foot of Crane. "We'll meet up there and then fan out and work our way westward toward French Hill. My pa and Carson Russell will be at that end, so if we scare up any deer, we'll drive them straight to where they'll be waiting."

Hollis nodded. That was a sensible plan. "They're the ones who shoot the deer?" he asked.

"Probably. Unless one of us who's driving is able to get off a clean shot. It doesn't matter who does the shooting, though. We all share the deer."

Hollis didn't ask any more questions for a while, using all his breath to trudge through the snow and focusing his attention on the southeast face of Crane, now revealed by the earliest rays of dawn. Several dark shadows striped the rocky facade, suggesting the presence of caves. He tried to memorize their location.

He was glad he hadn't attempted to hunt for the gold in this snow. It was rough going, and instead of being cold, as he'd expected, he was beginning to sweat. He loosened his scarf and undid his coat.

"Walk behind me for a bit," Gibby offered. "I'll break a trail for you." Hollis dropped back and found the going easier as he walked through the snow packed down by Gibby's big feet. It was light out by the time they reached the summit of the hill and stopped to catch their breath. They could hear the Pascos coming from the East, talking and laughing as they walked. A breeze stirred and Hollis shivered as its sharp fingers jabbed beneath his open coat.

"Best button up," Gibby said. "Once you stop moving, you get cold fast."

Hollis nodded. Already he felt chilled to the bone. He buttoned his coat, tightened his scarf, and sat on a stump with his back to the wind.

"Stand up," Gibby instructed him. "Swing your arms, stomp your feet. You gotta keep moving." Reluctantly Hollis did as he was told, and miraculously the feeling began to return to his fingers and toes. By the time the Pascos arrived he was once again comfortable.

"Boys," Gibby said, "This here's young Hollis, Johnny Ingraham's boy." The way he said it made Hollis feel special and, without realizing it, he straightened his shoulders. Then, for Hollis' benefit Gibby added, "Frank and Llew Pasco."

To Hollis' surprise, the "Pasco boys" were grown men, older than Gibby. Frank and Llew, he knew, were brothers, but they couldn't have looked much less alike. Frank was short and stout and had a ruddy complexion. He huffed and puffed as he walked and chuckled readily at comments made by the others. Llew was long and lean and pale, and seldom spoke or smiled, just nodding in response to comments directed his way.

"Well," Frank said, "Let's fan out and get those deer moving. We saw some sign on our way up the hill, so maybe luck will be with us."

"That's good news," Gibby responded. "We'll each keep the person on our right in sight. Hollis, you'll be on my right. We won't lose you, but if by some chance you do get separated from us, you be sure you stop and stay in one place."

Frank and Llew nodded. Frank said, "Remember the time that city feller got lost up on the mountain?"

The other men nodded, and Frank turned to Hollis. "He wandered around for hours and ended up miles from where he first got lost. We didn't know where to look for him."

Gibby concurred. "We were lucky to find him at all. A man who gets lost should stay put."

Hollis promised not to wander if they became separated, and the group spaced themselves about thirty yards apart and slowly but steadily began to work their way across the ridge. After about twenty minutes Llew snapped his rifle to his shoulder. Hollis' eyes followed the direction of the barrel just in time to see a huge buck poised on a small knoll looking at them. A shot rang out, and at that exact moment the buck whirled and disappeared into the woods.

"Did you get him?" Frank shouted.

Llew shook his head and lowered his gun in response.

"Well, he's long gone. No matter," Gibby assured him. "There'll be others."

Hollis couldn't help feeling secretly happy that the magnificent buck had gotten away.

They continued on their way, with an occasional remark or bit of banter shouted back and forth. After another half an hour or so, Frank drew their attention to a trampled area beneath a balsam tree with some deer tracks leading away from it. "Must've bedded down here for the night," he said.

The others agreed.

"Looks like two or three of 'em," he continued.

Gibby studied the tracks. "I make it two," he said. One of 'em has some size to it. And they appear to be headed straight toward Pa and Carson."

The Buck

With renewed energy they resumed their trek toward French Hill, following the tracks in the snow. About ten minutes later two shots pierced the quiet morning. Faintly they could hear a triumphant shout.

"Well, boys," said Frank, "there'll be venison in the pot tonight!" They picked up the pace then, walking together and exchanging stories of past hunting feats. Hollis soaked it all in, enjoying the companionship. Frank clapped him on the shoulder. "Not bad, son! Your first day out, and your party bags a deer. My first hunt, all I got was frostbite!"

Before long they emerged from the woods into a clearing where they found Ira Goodnow and Carson Russell busily gutting a large buck. The men seemed unmindful of the red blood soaking into the crisp white snow as they appreciatively discussed the size and weight of the deer and the number of points on the antlers. Hollis stood back, trying to sort through the mixture of emotions he was experiencing. He was happy that the hunt had been successful, yet sad for the deer with the beautiful brown eyes.

"You wanta drag it or carry it?" asked Gibby's father.

"It's got a lotta size to it. Best drag it?" responded Gibby, looking to the other men for confirmation.

"Drag it," they agreed, so Gibby and Frank Pasco each took a firm grip on an antler and proceeded to drag the buck on its back over the snow toward French Hill Road where the Goodnow's yoke of oxen patiently waited, hitched to a vehicle that looked like a farm wagon mounted on runners. Gibby and Frank set the buck down behind this sleigh, and Llew and Carson moved around to the hindquarters to hoist it onto the sleigh.

"Hollis, steady the oxen while we load up," Gibby said.

Hollis started toward the head of the near ox and was just reaching for the side of its halter when his foot hit a patch of ice and skated out from beneath him. The startled ox jerked its head and side-stepped quickly, jostling his teammate and causing it to lurch forward in alarm. Just as it seemed that the team might bolt before Hollis or any of the men could control them, a huge man dressed all in buckskin appeared seemingly out of nowhere and instantly calmed the animals, grasping their halters firmly and speaking softly to them in a language foreign to Hollis' ear. Still sprawled on the ground beside the oxen's sharp hoofs, he stared in amazement at this apparition. His long black hair blended with the black bearskin hat pulled down over his ears. Other hides were draped poncho-fashion over his shoulders. A large bone-handled hunting knife hung in a laced up leather sheath on the belt around his fringed buckskin shirt. Buckskin leggings and knee-high moccasins completed the picture. He held the oxen while the men hoisted the deer onto the sleigh.

"We're much obliged," said Gibby, coming around to the front of the sleigh.

The man said nothing, but gave a curt nod of his head. As suddenly and silently as he had appeared, he disappeared, slipping into a stand of hemlock saplings as though he had never been there.

Hollis stared open-mouthed after him. "Who was that?"

"That was Jock Centerbar," Gibby said.

Jock Centerbar! Nicholas' father! Hollis was startled. "How come he didn't say anything?"

"He don't have much to say—can't speak English good, I guess, and he's a loner," Llew volunteered. "Only time I ever heard him talk was down to the store trading hides for flour and such."

Hollis tried to understand. "But doesn't he have any friends?"

"Doesn't seem to want any," Frank said. "Him and his wife stay up on the hill with that brood of children. He hunts and traps for meat and fur, and his woman has a garden and gathers wild plants. Guess that's the Indian in her."

Hollis shook his head. It was hard to imagine this frightening man as the father of his friend Nicholas. He felt a little shiver as he thought of the strange man, never guessing the role that Jacques St. Hubert was to play in his life.

The next two weeks fairly flew by. The weather remained cold, preventing the snow from melting. A letter arrived from Ma, and Hollis took it up to his room to read in private. In it she told of her work at the hotel, and amusing stories about some of the guests. Hollis could tell that she was deliberately trying to make everything sound fun, but he worried about the long hours of hard work. It made him even more impatient to make his expedition to find the gold, but he knew he had to wait for a thaw. He wished he could tell her that help was coming. Instead he kept busy with his schoolwork and church and chores around the farm.

Before he knew it, Thanksgiving had arrived. Grandma was bustling around the kitchen long before dawn, filling the house with the aroma of fresh-baked pies and rolls, and simmering ham. About midmorning the Goodnows arrived. Gibby's mother, Julia Goodnow, was a tiny wren-like woman who carried a large basket covered with blue and white gingham. She was followed by her husband, Ira, who bore a freshly-plucked wild turkey and a venison steak. While Grandma and Grandpa welcomed the senior Goodnows, Gibby called Hollis out to their sleigh.

"Come see what I've brought you!" he said.

Hollis ran out and scrambled up onto one of the runners. On the floor of the sleigh he saw a large folded brown hide. "This is for me?" he asked in surprise.

"I thought you might like this as your share of the buck we got. If you stretch it and scrape it good you can sell it or trade it down to the store."

"I could get money for it?" he asked excitedly.

"Some. Not a lot," Gibby said. "You want me to show you what to do with it?"

"You bet I do! Thanks!" He didn't dare tell Gibby he had made other plans for raising money. Besides, this would tide him over until he could get up the mountain to find the gold.

Together they stretched the deer hide out and tacked it to the barn door, fur side in, and Gibby showed him how to scrape it to remove bits of fat and flesh.

By the time they returned to the house the smell of roasting turkey was permeating the kitchen, and the women had chased the men out onto the porch so the table could be set. Hollis and Gibby joined them while the older men smoked their pipes and discussed the year's crops and neighborhood news.

"Warm air's movin' in," Ira said after a lull in the conversation.

"That it is," Grandpa agreed, nodding wisely. "Wouldn't be surprised if all this snow will be gone in a couple a days. It'll make a mess of things, what with the mud and all."

Ira drew on his pipe. "Yep. I remember a warm spell we had one December. Must've been back in '50. Maybe '51. Stayed warm for over a week. We had such warm days the sap rose in the trees. Old Albert Pasco tapped his maples." Ira laughed. "Yep, it sure does feel like a warm spell comin' on."

Soon the door opened and Grandma announced that dinner was served. The table was so crowded with bowls and platters of food there was hardly room for their plates. In addition to the glazed ham, venison steak and golden turkey with gravy, there was a mountain of potatoes, Grandma's "leather britches" beans simmered to tenderness, soft yeast rolls, Julia's special peach preserves, sweet pickles and wild cranberry sauce. Grandpa asked the blessing and soon they were all passing and savoring the holiday treats, eating until they thought they would burst. The women cleared away the platters and bowls and replaced them with apple and pumpkin and mincemeat pies, along with a big pot of steaming coffee. Somehow they all managed to find room for pie and then lingered around the table sipping coffee. Grandma even let Hollis have some, although his cup contained more fresh farm cream than coffee.

It was Ira who finally broke the spell of contentment that had settled over the table. Pushing his chair back, he groaned, "We'd best be on our way. We have stock to do for at home."

Julia sighed and nodded. "Let me help Hazel clean up and I'll be ready to go."

Grandma put her hand on Julia's arm. "Nonsense! It'll be dark before long. You run along. Hollis will help me." She repacked Julia's basket with slices of leftover ham and turkey and slabs of pie. You be on your way."

"Thank you, Hazel. I guess the way the snow's been melting, we should hurry home while the sleigh can still make it through."

Hollis brought in water for Grandma to heat for the dishes and he and Grandpa went out to tend the livestock while Grandma put the food out on the porch to cool and washed up. Hollis proudly showed Grandpa the deer hide tacked to the barn door. "Gibby says when I finish scraping it and drying it, I can sell it at the store."

"You can sell it or trade it for goods."

"I'm selling it," Hollis declared decisively.

Grandpa snorted. "Doesn't surprise me."

They turned and went back up to the house. The unseasonably warm air smelled like spring and all around them trickles of melting snow chirped contentedly as they found their way to the creek.

Later that night, as Hollis lay on his bed, his eyes groping for the familiar silhouette of Crane, he thought about the warming weather. If this warm spell held, he would be able to go find the gold on Crane Mountain!

10

Searching for Treasure

Four days after Thanksgiving found the weather still warm. Most of the snow had melted, leaving thick, gooey mud in its place. Some patches of snow were still visible on Crane's face, but Hollis decided that if he hoped to climb the mountain before spring, he would have to make his move. He resolved to go the next morning, and all that day in school he could think of nothing else. He told no one of his plan until he got Nicholas alone that afternoon on their way home from school.

Nicholas reacted with amazement. "You're crazy!" he exclaimed. You'll catch it from Miss Kenyon for playing hooky, and I'll bet your Grandma and Grandpa won't look very kindly on it, either."

Hollis had thought it all out. "Miss Kenyon will just think I'm out sick. I'll make up the work I miss, and since I'll be home at the usual time, Grandma and Grandpa won't know, either. Unless I bring home the gold, that is."

Nicholas shook his head. "How are you going to find it in that cave when no one else has been able to?"

"I don't know. I just know that I've gotta find it, to send to my ma. Besides, there could be other caves. I think I've seen some, on the east side."

"Well, I still say you're crazy."

"Just promise you won't tell anyone."

"I promise. Good luck."

Good luck was with Hollis the next morning. He awoke early and was able to sneak his bag of supplies downstairs and out to the cover of the maple tree without being heard. He hurriedly completed his chores, washed up and went into the house for breakfast. He was so excited about the expedition he was about to take that several times he found his mouth open ready to talk about it. Catching himself, he'd quickly stuff in some more food.

"My, you're as hungry as a bear!" Grandma said as he downed his third biscuit.

Hollis nodded as he washed it down with half a glass of milk. "Okay if I take a couple of these to eat on the way to school?" Ordinarily the lie would have stuck in his throat, but today it was just a necessary part of his glorious adventure.

"Take as many as you want. That's what they're for."

He stuffed three inside his shirt, pulled on his coat and grabbed his dinner pail. "Bye!" he shouted as he ran out the door.

He was halfway up French Hill when he heard the Centerbar children coming down on their way to school. He knew that Nicholas would not betray him, but he couldn't trust the younger children to be able to keep his secret. He ducked behind a smooth gray beech tree until they were well past him. That way they could tell Miss Kenyon in all honesty that they had not seen him that morning. As soon as they were gone, he turned and climbed the hill they had just come down.

In about a mile he came to a place Nicholas had described to him, the spot where the road crested French Hill and forked. The left branch, he knew, went to the four corners at Johnsburg, and the right branch was the trail up the mountain. Excitement surged through him as he proceeded along the Johnsburg route. After about half a mile of trudging he came to another fork. This was the path to the pond that Nicholas had told him about. He took the right fork and began watching for the cave. Just a few yards down this path he spotted some boulders with a black hole at the base. This was the entrance to the cave! Hollis tossed his sack down and threw himself on his belly to peer into the opening. Far off he could see a thin shaft of light coming from an opening at the other end of the cave. Finding it too dark to see, he scrambled to get a candle stub out of the sack and matches out of his pants pocket. Lighting the candle, he carefully inched his way through the cave entrance and looked around.

He could see nothing that looked like gold, but of course he had known it wouldn't be out in plain sight, or, as Nicholas and Tommy had pointed out, somebody would have found it by now. Still on his belly, he backed out and reached for his sack of supplies, pulling them back into the cave with him. He extracted the broken shovel. Digging was going to be more difficult than he anticipated, since nowhere in this long narrow tunnel was there a spot with enough headroom to even sit up, let alone stand up. Propping himself up on his left elbow, he found a small crevice in which to wedge the candle and began awkwardly wielding the shovel. Clang! Clang! Clang! The shovel unearthed nothing, for the floor of the cave was frozen solid. Refusing to be discouraged, Hollis picked up the candle, and, dragging the sack, wormed his way through the cave inspecting every crack and crevice for a hidden chamber that might house the treasure. Nothing looked the least bit promising.

No matter. He hadn't really expected to find the gold in this cave. It was too easy. He blew out the candle as he emerged from the far side of the cave. It was still early. He would have plenty of time to find other caves and explore them.

He stood up and looked at the mountain. He had not seen this side of it before. From his bedroom window he had studied the east side of Crane, mentally noting dark shadows on its face that might be caves. He decided that was the best bet, and set out to circle a quarter of the way around the base of the mountain and then work his way up the east side. The going was rough, since there was no trail in that direction, and he had to scramble over rocks and fallen trees, and leap across little rivulets. It was farther than he had expected.

The sun was high in the sky by the time he found himself staring up the east side of the mountain. It was at the same time familiar and strange, for its whole character changed at close range. The simple little zig-zaggy routes up the mountain he had plotted from his window were now complicated rocky outcroppings with little to offer for hands or toes to grip. He took off his coat, stuffed it into the sack and sat down on a rock to eat some biscuits and puzzle over the situation. At last he spied a place where several scrawny trees had managed to take root along a diagonal slope up the lower side of the east face. Perhaps with his rope he could use the trees to work his way up along that groove in the rock.

He dusted the crumbs off his hands and knelt by one of the many little streams of melted snow to scoop up a few swallows of water. As he stood to leave, he slipped on some wet leaves and plopped down into the water. In spite of himself, he laughed. This was how his gold hunt had begun; maybe it was a good sign. His pant legs were wet, but what did that matter on a warm day like this?

Distances on the mountain were deceptive. It was an hour or more before Hollis had worked his way to the beginning of the series of trees, which, he discovered, were much further apart than they had appeared while he was munching his biscuits. He took the coil of rope from his sack and hung it over his shoulder. He pulled up two ears at the top of his sack and tied them together, leaving enough of an opening to thread his belt through it. The sack banged annoyingly against his legs as he walked, but he knew he would need both hands free to make the ascent.

Slowly he began the arduous climb, sometimes wedging his foot against a rock or tree, and other times grasping at flimsy roots and twigs. He had hoped to be able to toss the rope around the trunk of a tree ahead of him and pull himself up, but that didn't work. Sometimes his only recourse was to dig his hands into the gravelly dirt or patches of granular snow and claw his way up. His fingers were soon scratched and bleeding, his trouser knees torn, but as long as he could keep moving forward he didn't care. Hope energized him.

At last he reached a small flat spot where the trees ended, and he sat down to plan his next move. As he rested, a small breeze sprang up and caused him to shiver. He would be warm as soon as he started moving again. But where to move to? He stood. To his left a rocky ledge about six inches wide made a narrow passageway along a massive wall of rock. With his body flattened against the side of the cliff, his fingers clawing anything that protruded, Hollis cautiously inched his way sideways up the sloping ledge. His progress was slow, and he was becoming quite chilled. Donning his coat on the ledge was out of the question, so he tried to think about the gold instead. Surely the gold was here, and he would soon be triumphantly bringing it home!

He had seen a vertical crack in the face of the cliff about four feet above the ledge and twenty feet to his left, and he focused on reaching that spot. Gradually the ledge widened until, at the spot where it widened to a foot, it ended abruptly. Hollis peered over the edge and gasped as he saw the ground far below him. He realized for the first time how high he had climbed and how dangerous his position had become.

He wrenched his gaze away from the foot of the cliff and turned his attention to the crack. It would be a great place to hide a treasure! From his place on the ledge he couldn't quite see into the twelve-inch-wide crevice, so he eagerly hauled himself up for a view of the interior. Bitter disappointment engulfed him then, for there was no hidden treasure, no gold, no sign of man whatsoever. There was nothing there but cold, hard, unforgiving rock.

Hollis hadn't known until that moment how much he had counted on the gold's being there. Finding the crevice empty knocked the wind out of him. He slumped back down on the ledge, tired and discouraged. And cold. He pulled his coat from the sack and put it on, buttoning it up to his chin. All this for nothing! Just like Nicholas had said, there was no gold; it was just a story for little children.

There was nothing to do but retrace his steps to the foot of the cliff, a job that was more difficult than he had expected. As he took his first step a small pebble rolled beneath his foot, causing him to lose his balance and lurch perilously close to the edge of the cliff. His eyes leaped to the jumble of rocks at its base. One more misstep could cost his life. He clung to the rock wall, paralyzed. His heart pounded in his ears and he felt unable to draw a breath. As he extended his foot, his knees trembled as though they would buckle beneath him. He forced himself to look only at the ledge, averting his eyes from the chasm below. With agonizing slowness he edged along his narrow path. When he finally reached the beginning of the ledge he stopped to catch his breath.

Alarm seized him as he saw that the afternoon sun had already dipped far behind the mountain. The ground below him was engulfed in deep shadows, and a new bite in the air made him shiver. "Got to hurry!" he thought, and began a tree-to-tree descent of the lower slope, hanging onto the first tree, while extending himself full length on his back until he could stretch no further. He slid recklessly on his backside until he crashed into the next tree down the slope. Unmindful of the scrapes and bruises he was acquiring, he continued this way until he reached the base of the cliff.

He turned back toward the trail he had left on the south side of the mountain. Occasionally he could spot his tracks in the snow he had marched so triumphantly across that morning, but it was getting harder and harder to see them, and harder and harder to know which way to go. He stopped and looked around him in the gathering darkness. He reminded himself that as long as he kept the mountain on his right side he was heading in the right direction. He could still see Crane looming against the yellow-orange sky that was rapidly filling with clouds blowing in from the northwest. He turned up his collar, shrinking down into his coat. If only he hadn't fallen into the creek. His legs and feet were freezing. He had to keep going! He continued on, struggling to make out landmarks in the gathering gloom. He changed direction to skirt a large fallen tree and found himself going steeply downhill.

Had he come up this hill in the morning? Was that tree there? He couldn't remember; this morning his head had been full of gold. He tried to correct his direction, but now Crane Mountain had been swallowed up in darkness. Which way to go? He began to run wildly in no particular direction, panic nipping at his heels. His toe caught under an exposed tree root and sent him sprawling face down of the forest floor, his lungs screaming for air.

He was hopelessly lost. Fear, frustration, pain and disappointment released a flood of tears. He didn't know how long he lay on the ground but slowly his sobs subsided and he sat up and rubbed his eyes. He got up gingerly, suddenly aware of every scrape, bruise and aching muscle. He knew he couldn't find his way out of the woods in the darkness. Perhaps later, when the moon came up....

Hollis threw down his sack in total frustration. No moonlight would get through those clouds. He kicked the sack angrily. It was so stupid to come here! He had to think, had to make a plan. Light, that was what he needed. Crawling on his hands and knees, he felt around in the darkness for his sack. His hands touched metal; it was the hatchet. Evidently the contents of the bag had spilled, so he groped around until he had found them all—the shovel, the rope and the sack, which still held his dinner pail and two of the candle stubs. The idea of candlelight comforted him, so he explored the terrain until he felt a large rock with a flattish top nearby. Onto this rock he placed the stubs, and then reached into his pocket for the wooden matches. Even before he pulled them out he knew he had a problem. His fall into the stream had soaked not only his trousers, but the matches as well. He tried to strike one on the rock anyway. Instead of making a sharp scratching noise, the match crumbled noiselessly across the stone, emitting a strong sulfur smell. Hollis spread the rest of the matches on the rock in the faint hope that somehow they would dry enough to light. Maybe, he thought, he could light a fire to warm himself.

That thought motivated Hollis to begin groping for twigs and branches, which he carefully piled for a fire. He never moved more than a few feet from his rock. Gibby's words echoed in his ears. "A man who gets lost oughta stay put and worry about staying warm." After gathering a nice stack of it he wanted to curl into a little ball and rest until the matches dried, but Gibby's advice prodded him again. He reluctantly stood up and began to stamp his feet and swing his arms. Slowly the chill began to leave him, and he dared to take a break. Sitting down on the ground, he puzzled over how he would be able to keep warm all night. He certainly couldn't jump around until dawn, but already he could feel the cold creeping back into his bones. Maybe he could improvise a little shelter to protect himself. He pulled himself to his feet again.

Tucking the hatchet into the waist of his trousers, he tied one end of the rope to a sapling next to his rock and the other end to his wrist. Then he began a methodical hands-and-knees exploration of the area around the rock. The blackness of the night was relentless. Hollis could see only by means of his fingertips. Rock, more rocks, a moss-covered stump, smooth-barked saplings and shaggy-barked older trees met his touch. At last there was something different—branches full of soft needles—balsam or spruce, judging from the smell. With the help of the hatchet Hollis began ripping the small branches from their trunk, piling them by his knees. By the time he had run out of boughs that he could reach, he had a sizable mound. Wrapping his arms around them he stood and haltingly made his was back to the rock, using the rope to guide him. He moved around the rock until he discovered the side most sheltered from the rising wind, and set about making his den. He first laid a thick layer of branches on the ground to keep out the cold when he sat. Next he leaned the rest of the branches up against the side of the rock in a semicircular arrangement, forming a crude hut. The project had brightened his mood, and he crawled almost happily into his shelter to try it out. It was far from warm, but definitely more cozy than the open air. He could rest awhile.

He dozed fitfully, dreaming strange dreams. He was very cold. He dreamed that he was fighting his way through a dark forest with growth so thick he couldn't see anything except tree branches all around him. He tried to move, pushing branches out of his way like a swimmer swimming upstream. On and on he went. Was there no end to this forest? Suddenly he burst out of the woods into a bright clearing. Standing in the middle of the clearing was a huge buck, with sunlight glistening off its radiant coat. To his surprise, the buck turned and looked at him, saying, "Sleep now."

Some time later Hollis awoke with a start in total darkness. He was cold and stiff and confused. The smell of evergreen boughs reminded him of his predicament. He forced himself to unbend his curled-up legs and crawl out of the relative warmth of his nest into the cold night air to exercise again. He wondered how late it was. Even more than that, he wondered what Grandma and Grandpa must be thinking by now.

11

Rescue on the Mountain

Sanford Ingraham waited almost until dark to go out to the barns to do the milking and start chores. He wouldn't ever have let on, but he had come to enjoy sharing that time with Hollis, teaching him the tricks of farming and seeing how quickly he learned. He admired Hollis' ability to see without being told what chores needed to be done, and his thoroughness in doing them. He noticed that Hollis was no longer struggling so hard when he carried the buckets from the creek, and was proud to see how much stronger he was becoming. He had a way with the animals, and had even learned to clean out the giant hoofs of Jackie and Gwen. Where was he? He was exceptionally late today, and Grandpa frowned, wondering if the boy had again been kept after school.

As if Hazel had read his thoughts, she said, "I'm sure he's just off playing with Tommy or Nicholas. You know how boys lose all track of time."

Grandpa did not miss the little lines of worry on her forehead, so he decided against telling her about the bear tracks he had seen down the lane earlier that afternoon, the bear evidently having been lured out of hibernation by the recent warm weather. It would be unusual for a black bear to bother a human, but if it was hungry enough and the human carried a dinner pail...Grandpa shook the thought from his head. "I'll be starting the chores," he said. "Send the boy on down to the barn when he gets here."

Chores completed, he returned to the house to find Grandma worriedly pacing the kitchen. "I'm sure there's nothing to worry about," she said, as much to convince herself as her husband. "They probably just stopped off at the frog pond. But the temperature's dropping, and it's getting so late!" she said.

Grandpa patted her shoulder. "I'll hitch up the team and go have a look. You keep supper hot, for we'll be hungry when we get home."

In a few minutes he was on his way, the kerosene lanterns glowing on either side of his wagon. Cold weather was moving in and he hunched down inside his coat. He had gone just a quarter of a mile down Mill Creek Road when he met up with Gibby, headed toward him on horseback. They both reined to a halt.

"'Sanford, that you?" Gibby asked. "Your boy taken a turn for the worse, has he?"

"A turn for the worse? What do you mean?" Grandpa asked.

"I've just come from Websters. Tommy said Hollis was out sick today. I thought maybe you were going to fetch a doctor, you being out so late and all."

Grandpa shook his head. "The boy left for school as usual this morning. You mean he never got there?" he asked with thinly disguised alarm.

"Not according to Tom."

"Then I'm going up to talk to young Centerbar and see if he's seen him," Grandpa said, wheeling the team and wagon around in the road.

"It's a cold night for a boy to be out on his own," Gibby said with concern. "I'll go collect a few men in case we need to send out a search party. And I'll pick up some supplies and take Ma down to set with Hazel."

Without waiting for a thank you, Gibby spurred his horse to a gallop and disappeared into the night. Grandpa resisted the impulse to speed the gait of his team. They would need to save their energy for the steep climb up French Hill. It felt like hours before he was knocking at the door of the Centerbars' small log cabin. From within he could hear a young voice exclaim in surprise, "Mama, there's someone at the door!"

In a moment the door opened, revealing a young woman with long black braids. Her slender form was garbed in a brown buckskin dress. A dark-eyed little girl peered out from behind her skirt. "Yes?" the woman asked.

"Ma'am," Grandpa said, "I'm looking for my boy—my grandson, Hollis. Name's Sanford Ingraham, Ma'am," he added awkwardly, remembering his manners.

"And I am *Étoile*–'Star', as you say. There is no boy here—except my own sons," she said, gesturing toward the little knot of children hanging back. Something in Nicholas' demeanor stirred the mother's intuition in Star. "Nicholas," she said sharply, "what do you know of this boy?"

Nicholas stepped forward, fear and uncertainty causing him to stammer at first. "I-I thought he'd be all right. He promised he'd be back before dark."

"Back? Back from where?" Grandpa pressed him.

"Back from the mountain."

"You'd better come in," Star Centerbar said, guiding Grandpa into the room and closing the door.

"He had this crazy idea that he could find the lost gold on the mountain," Nicholas continued. "I tried to tell him it was no use, but he said he had to find it for his Ma. And he said he'd be back before dark."

His mother wrung her hands anxiously. "You should have stopped him."

"'Should have' doesn't matter now," Grandpa cut in. "We have to find him. Did he say where he was going to look?"

"He was going to look first in the cave on the trail to the pond—you know the one?"

Grandpa nodded.

"Then he said something about checking for caves on the east side of the mountain."

For the first time that day Grandpa felt terror grip the pit of his stomach. As a boy he had played along the slopes at the foot of the rocky eastern face of Crane. On a few occasions he had made ill-advised attempts to reach the alluring crevices that creased those

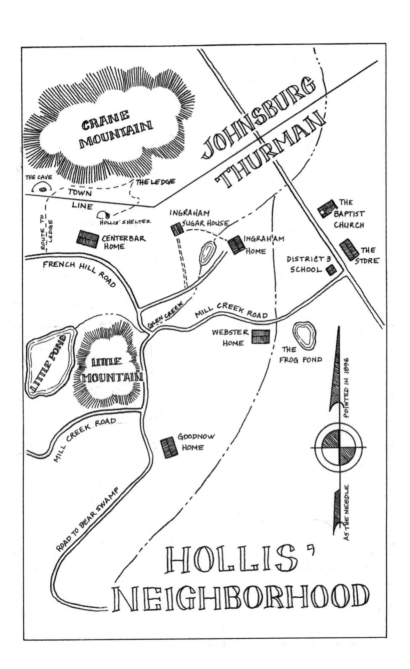

CRANE MOUNTAIN

JOHNSBURG

THURMAN

THE CAVE

TOWN LINE

THE LEDGE

HOLLIS' SHELTER

ROUTE TO LEDGE

INGRAHAM SUGAR HOUSE

CENTERBAR HOME

INGRAHAM HOME

THE BAPTIST CHURCH

DISTRICT 3 SCHOOL

THE STORE

FRENCH HILL ROAD

GLEN CREEK

MILL CREEK ROAD

LITTLE POND

LITTLE MOUNTAIN

WEBSTER HOME

THE FROG POND

MILL CREEK ROAD

GOODNOW HOME

POINTED IN 1896

AS THE NEEDLE

ROAD TO BEAR SWAMP

HOLLIS'
NEIGHBORHOOD

cliffs. The memory of the dangerous precipices was so sharp it sucked his breath away and he sagged against the door. "I've got to find him!" he said hoarsely.

Star put her hand sympathetically on his arm. "It is bad that he is there, but you cannot go. It is not wise in this darkness. And even if you do find him, how will you bring him out of the woods? It is not wise."

Grandpa nodded. "All the same," he said stubbornly, "I have to go. I have to know that he isn't lying at the foot of one of those cliffs. There'll be others coming along to search—Gibby Goodnow and them. I'll thank you to tell them where I've gone."

He was about to open the door when Jock Centerbar, who had been standing in the shadows at the rear of the cabin, stepped into the light. The expression on his face showed that he had understood most of what had been said. In a low voice he addressed Grandpa in French. *"Il faut que vous restiez ici. J'irai."*

Grandpa looked questioningly at Mrs. Centerbar.

"You must stay," she translated. "My husband will go." Then she added, by way of argument, "It is better, you know. My husband knows these woods well and he is strong. He can move quickly. You wait here for your friends and show them the way to go."

Grandpa knew that Jock Centerbar could travel through the woods twice as fast as he could, so he reluctantly agreed. "Take one of my horses, at least as far as the trail," he said to Jock. "And take a lantern."

Jock nodded, quickly pulling on his fur hat and cape. "I go now."

"God speed you," Grandpa said.

Star motioned Grandpa toward a chair by the fireplace. It was made of saplings lashed together with rawhide, and the seat and back were made of tautly-stretched hides. "Sit," she said kindly. "We must be patient. I will fix you some tea."

He sat in front of the fireplace, wishing to be in the woods, wishing to have two strong legs, wishing to be young enough and healthy enough to do what needed doing. Star placed a hot tin cup in his hand and he sipped at the steaming herbal concoction sweetened with honey. He wondered how long it had been since the boy had eaten or drunk.

He stared into the flames for what seemed like hours. The Centerbar children quietly climbed the ladder to the loft and went to bed. Mrs. Centerbar added some logs to the fire, drew a stool up beside it and began lacing together a moccasin. "For Jean-Paul," she said, catching his glance. "These boys grow like fawns."

A shadow crossed Grandpa's face as he thought of his boy, the son of his son, alone in the cold dark woods.

"Don't worry," Star said. "Jacques St. Hubert will find him."

Jacques St. Hubert—Jock Centerbar—was able to ride the horse as far as the first cave, where he found Hollis' tracks leading away toward the east. Dismounting, he tied the horse and began to follow the tracks, a difficult job, despite his skill and the lantern. Occasionally, due to rocks, he lost the trail and had to work in circles until he could pick it up again. Nearly three hours passed before the tracks led him to the foot of the cliff. He held the lantern high and studied the scuffs on the tree-lined slope that Hollis had skidded down some hours before. At long last he saw what he had been hoping to find, a set of footprints leading away from the cliff's base. But where were they headed? For fifteen or twenty minutes he followed them southward. Then they abruptly turned to the east and then to the south again. The erratic path Hollis had taken in the deepening dusk made Jacques' task more difficult, but he followed the trail tenaciously for another hour. He knew the dangers of cold and darkness to one lost in the woods. And this was a boy younger and smaller than his own Nicholas.

Suddenly Jacques saw the bright gleam of something metal in his lantern light. He bent down to inspect the source and found the broken shovel. Near it he spotted the hatchet and a neatly coiled rope. He found the candle stubs and a row of wet matches on the rock, but no boy. He circled the rock and nearly tripped over the hemlock boughs piled against it. "'Ollis!" he called.

A soft moan at his feet startled him. He dropped to his knees and tore at the branches, uncovering Hollis.

"Ah! Mon Dieu! Tu as froid!" he exclaimed, scooping Hollis up in his arms and holding him against his chest under the fur drapes. "Cold! So cold!"

He managed to loop the lantern handle over his wrist and set off through the woods with giant strides toward the spot where he had left Grandpa's horse.

*   *   *

Back at the Centerbar cabin Grandpa was jolted out of fitful dozing by the clatter of horses in the yard. He pulled himself clumsily to his feet. Star Centerbar was already at the door with a candle. It was Gibby, with Bob Webster and Carson Russell, all on horseback. Behind them came a wagon bearing Ira and Julia Goodnow and Grandma.

"Any news of the boy?" Gibby asked, putting words to the question on everyone's mind.

"He's been out on the mountain since morning," Grandpa said. "Jock Centerbar set out after him some time back. He was going to start at the old cave and then work eastward."

Grandpa reached up to help Grandma down from the wagon. "Hazel, what are you doing here?"

"I had to come," she said. "And besides, you men can't go off into the woods on empty stomachs. Julia and I packed some food."

Mrs. Centerbar opened the door wider.

"Please come in out of the cold to make your plan."

Hazel and Julia carried three large baskets into the cabin and the men dismounted and followed, taking care to kick the mud from their boots and remove their hats before entering. A row of little heads appeared at the edge of the loft, but the children knew better than to come down.

Gibby unrolled a sketch of the mountain and its trails. He held a candle over it and jabbed with his finger at a place labeled "cave". "The way I see it," he said, "we take the horses to here and then split into pairs, each pair on foot with a lantern. We'll fan out and work our way—"

Before he could finish the thought, the door to the cabin burst open. Jock Centerbar stood framed in the doorway with Hollis in his arms.

"Praise the Lord!" was all Grandma could say, and Grandpa was speechless.

Gibby hurried to relieve Jock of his burden, but the woodsman brushed past him to place Hollis on some hides beside the fire. He rubbed his wrists and feet briskly while Star poured a cup of her hot tea. She handed it to Hazel, smiling. "Have him sip this slowly," she said gently. "It will warm him on the inside."

Grandma took it gratefully and knelt beside Hollis. Propping his head up on her knees, she held the cup to his lips, urging him to drink. He was somewhat dazed but able to take small swallows. Between sips she could hear him mumbling, "I will lift up mine eyes...."

"You hush now. Drink this and rest," she said.

"Ze cold, it near finish ze boy," Jock said haltingly to Grandma. "'E be good now." Satisfied that Hollis was on the mend and in good hands, he stood.

Grandpa moved away from the group of men and approached Jock. "Centerbar, I don't know how to thank you. You and your wife have been real good neighbors to us. If there's ever anything–any way we can ever...." His words trailed off awkwardly.

Jock nodded, obviously uncomfortable with this show of gratitude. Just then Hollis' voice distracted them. "Grandma, is that your basket? I'm starving!"

Jock's usually stern face split into a grin, and he bellowed, "'*Ollis, il a faim!*'" He burst into belly-shaking guffaws, and the rest of the group, even Grandpa, joined in, relief apparent in all their faces. Grandma and Julia spread out the contents of the baskets, and the table groaned under the load of cheese, bread and preserves, dried fruit, hard-boiled eggs, jerky and fried chicken. "Looks like our search party rations turned into a celebration supper," Grandma said to Star. Then she nodded to the loft where six sparkling-eyed faces still peeked down. "Think they'd like to join the party?" she asked. Star smiled at her brood, who couldn't have scrambled down the ladder faster.

Nicholas, the last to descend, made his way through the laughing, chattering crowd of neighbors to Hollis' side. "Listen, Hollis," he began, "I'm really sorry."

"Forget it," Hollis said. "You had to tell them where I was."

"Not that!" Nicholas said. "I'm sorry I didn't talk you out of going in the first place!"

"Yeah," Hollis said ruefully, "you should have told me there was no gold hidden on the mountain."

Nicholas had opened his mouth to protest indignantly when he saw a grin tugging at the corners of Hollis' mouth. He punched Hollis playfully in the shoulder. "You idiot!"

Grandma and Julia and Star began dishing up the food, and they all ate heartily. Grandma declared that it was like the miracle of the fishes and the loaves. Ira said it put him in mind of their younger days when they would all get together for a barn-raising and celebrate with food and music late into the night after the work was done.

"Yup," he said, "We used-ta could sing and dance till one or two in the morning, walk home and get up at five to do another full day's work. I miss those days. And, Sanford," he said, turning to Grandpa, "I miss hearing you play that fiddle!" To Jock and Star he said, "Why, this man could play fiddle like you never heard. I can remember reels so fast they'd take the wind right out of you, and ballads so purty they'd make the hair stand right up on the back of your neck."

"That's the truth," Julia agreed. "You really ought to pick it up again, Sanford."

Grandpa raised his hand in protest. "Those days are long gone," he said, shaking his head. "And that fiddle's in worse shape than I am!"

His friends all laughed and resumed their visiting, and Hollis felt an insistent tug on his sleeve. "Hollis!"

"Yes, Jean-Paul?" Hollis responded patiently.

"Did you find that gold?"

"No, Jean-Paul. I'm afraid there is no gold. It was just a story, and believing that story almost got me killed."

"Speaking of getting killed," Nicholas said in a low voice, "what are your grandparents going to do to you?"

Hollis sucked his breath between his teeth. "I guess I'll find out," was all he said.

12

Holiday Secrets

Grandma and Grandpa were surprisingly calm about his disappearing act, although they made it abundantly clear that he was never to play hooky again, and never to go off to the mountain by himself again. He had expected Grandpa to be furious, but the funny thing was, Grandpa hardly had a word to say about the subject, and no longer seemed so mean and sour. Sometimes he actually talked to Hollis when he didn't have to, and, once in a while, Hollis caught him smiling. It was almost as though he didn't hate having him around anymore.

Just to make sure that Hollis wouldn't wander off, Grandma and Grandpa kept him about twice as busy around home. First there was the letter he had to write to Ma, telling her of his foolishness, assuring her that he was all right, and promising never to do such a thing again. This time he didn't hide anything. He told Ma the whole story, from start to finish. He began with how he had been determined to earn money to help her pay off the debts and went on to tell about finding the fool's gold in the creek, and then told of his trip up the mountain, being lost and getting rescued. He wrapped it up by saying, "I still plan to earn some money, but don't worry about me searching for gold again. I'm going to see if I can find someone who needs work done after school. Your loving son, Hollis."

"Are you done?" Grandma asked. "I've got an envelope all

addressed. I'll see it goes out tomorrow." Hollis was so preoccupied with the problem of earning money that he didn't see Grandma slip a small folded note into the envelope with his letter just before she sealed it.

How was he going to earn some money? It was the same question he had been asking himself ever since Ma had sent him off that September morning with Gibby, and he didn't seem any closer to a solution now than he had been then. He wasn't afraid of hard work, but he didn't think the few odd jobs he would be able to get would earn enough to help Ma very much. If only he weren't just a boy!

His father would have been able to think of something; why couldn't he? Suddenly an image of the sugarhouse flashed into Hollis' mind. There was the doorway, and inside the crates of tins waiting to be filled, all labeled "Ingraham & Ingraham, Thurman, New York, Pure Maple Syrup." His mind began to race, and Gibby's words echoed in his ears. "Ingraham syrup was the best syrup around." Was there any way he could persuade Grandpa to open up the sugarhouse and make syrup again? Would he let Hollis help for a small share of the profits?

The more he thought about it, the more excited he became. The excitement, he realized, was caused, not only by the fact that he could finally earn money, but also by the idea of being half of "Ingraham & Ingraham," of inheriting and sharing his father's dream. He had to talk to Grandpa about it, but when? And how? He knew he would have to wait for the perfect time. Right now he had other jobs to do.

After writing to Ma, he had to write a letter to Miss Kenyon, apologizing for skipping school, promising never to do it again, and throwing himself on her mercy. Grandma had him copy it over three times before she was satisfied with the content, the spelling, the punctuation, and the penmanship. Miss Kenyon was surprisingly lenient, punishing Hollis only by assigning him extra reading, "Voyage to Lilliput" from *Gulliver's Travels*.

When he wasn't going to school or writing letters or reading the book (which, to his surprise, he enjoyed), he was doing chores. There were the usual barn chores, carrying in wood and hauling water. He had gotten much stronger, and could now carry two full buckets of water from the creek or pump without stopping to rest halfway. In addition to his daily tasks, he was performing extra jobs for Grandma and Grandpa. He shelled butternuts, oiled tools, mended the chickens' nesting boxes, fetched pumpkins from the root cellar, packed extra hay around the foundation to keep out the cold, and acted as Grandma's right-hand man on her special projects.

One day it was reorganizing the pantry and wiping down all the shelves. Another day she got a "bee in her bonnet," as Grandpa liked to say, to clear out the guest room and hang fresh wallpaper in it and paint the trim. When it was all done and the furniture replaced, Hollis had to admit that it looked very pretty. "But you never have any company," he said. "Who will ever see it?"

Grandma smiled a secretive little smile and said, "Well, we haven't taken our turn at putting up the schoolmarm."

Hollis was stunned. He knew that Miss Kenyon boarded around with local families, a month or so at each house, but the thought of her staying here, in his house, was an idea that had never occurred to him. "Miss Kenyon? Staying here?" he squeaked with alarm. "When?"

"Oh," said Grandma vaguely, "sometime. Maybe after Christmas."

Christmas was not far off, and preparations were very much on everybody's mind, especially since the weather had turned cold again and fresh snow covered the ground. One afternoon after school Grandma instructed Hollis to help her get some things she needed from the storeroom.

"I've got a sight of things to do before Christmas and I've got to get started."

By the time she had found the yarn, odds and ends of fabric remnants and sewing notions she needed, she decided the room needed a "good going over." They worked the better part of the afternoon tidying shelves, organizing, and dusting. It was then that Hollis got a truly wonderful idea. He dared not mention it to Grandma, but smiled with delight at his own genius.

There was scarcely a moment from then until Christmas when Grandma was not busy. By day she baked special cakes and cook-

ies and pies for gifts to neighbors. In the evening she knitted and
sewed into the late hours, long after Hollis had gone to bed.

Hollis had some secret projects of his own. To his surprise,
Grandpa suggested that they might work on a little carpentry project together in the barn, an undertaking they were careful to keep
secret from Grandma. When they weren't working on it they hid it
under some burlap grain bags behind a stack of chicken crates.

It was during one of these work sessions that Hollis confided to
Grandpa that he didn't know what to give his mother for Christmas.
"Gibby said he'd take it to her next time he takes a load of firewood
into Warrensburg," he said, "but I don't know what to give her. I
mean, I can't give her gold like I thought, so I've got to figure out
what she'd like."

Grandpa hesitated. "Well, I don't know about your ma, but most
women like pretty things," he said, stroking his beard. "They like
pretty things and sentimental things."

Hollis seemed doubtful. "Like what?"

"Oh, like a pretty picture, or—" A flash of inspiration lit up
Grandpa's face. "I know the very thing! Follow me, before it gets
dark!" Hurriedly they stashed the carpentry project behind the
crates and went outdoors, Grandpa with his cane in the lead, heading for the small stand of trees out behind the barn. "Cows killed
these trees by gnawing all the bark off around them," he said. "I've
been meaning to cut them down and saw them for firewood, but
now I'm glad I didn't. Look there!"

Hollis' eyes followed the line of his pointing finger and rested
on a strange shelf-like protrusion attached to the trunk of the tree
about eight feet off the ground.

"I spotted that two, maybe three years ago and clean forgot
about it. I think it's grown since then."

"It" was flat and whitish on the bottom, generally semicircular
in appearance, but with a slightly scalloped border. "What is it?"
Hollis asked, perplexed.

"They say that's a kind of mushroom, but when you finish with
it, it will be a work of art. Can you climb up there and pull it off the
tree?"

Hollis climbed up, and, resting his weight on one of the lower branches, prepared to wrest the mushroom from the host tree. "Just touch the sides, not the bottom!" Grandpa warned.

Hollis grasped it as told and gave a few tentative tugs.

"Put some muscle into it!"

Hollis gave an enormous pull, the tree gave up its prize, almost causing Hollis lose his balance and fall. He managed to catch himself, but the mushroom flew from his fingers. Luckily it dropped into Grandpa's arms. Hollis shinnied down the tree for a better look.

"This is a fine mushroom." Grandpa said admiringly. "You get yourself a nice sharp stick and draw on it. It will be a beautiful gift for your mother. Let's go show your Grandma."

Grandma was duly impressed with the mushroom, complimenting them on its size and shape. "This will make a fine gift," she pronounced, adding in a nostalgic tone, looking over Hollis' head at Grandpa, "Why, in my day, sometimes a young man would decorate one of these all pretty and give it to the girl he was sparkin'. Sometimes he'd write a bit of verse on it."

Grandpa snorted, blushing slightly, "The boy doesn't want to hear about such nonsense as that!"

Hollis giggled and ran upstairs to plan his design. Sitting on his bed in the lamplight with a scrap of paper and a pencil, he pondered over what to draw. From force of habit his eyes wandered to the window and the familiar profile of the mountain. Hurriedly he began sketching—first the big rounded hump on the left, and then the more distant peak rising from behind the right side of the hump, gradually sloping off the right and tapering out of sight. As he sketched, it grew too dark to see the mountain clearly, so he added from memory the soft lines of the low hills in the foreground.

After supper Grandpa sharpened a stick, and Hollis carefully etched his design on the mushroom's creamy white surface. When the mountain and hills were done, there remained a large blank space in the foreground. He felt his hand, almost of its own accord, inscribe a message on that space.

"Oh, my, that's perfect!" Grandma exclaimed, showing it to Grandpa. "Just perfect. We'll have to get some pretty tissue paper to wrap it in."

That Saturday Hollis rode to the Kenyontown store with his grandparents. Grandma packed up some butter and eggs to trade with Mr. Pasco, the storekeeper, and Hollis loaded the deer hide on the wagon, as well. The store shelves were stuffed with special holiday supplies. Grandma gravitated to the fabric counter to admire a new shipment of ribbon that had arrived and exchange pleasantries with the other ladies shopping there while Grandpa and Hollis took the trading goods to the counter to show the store keeper.

"Hmmm." said Mr. Pasco thoughtfully as he inspected the hide. It's a good big one, and you did a nice job of scraping it, too. Young man," he said with a friendly smile, "I think we can do business. Come up front, and I'll get you your money."

"Keep the money for a few minutes, sir," Hollis said. "I have to buy—" He caught himself and stopped abruptly. "Something," he concluded lamely.

"Well, you just look around," said Mr. Pasco.

"I'll go keep a rein on your Grandma," said Grandpa, "before she buys the place out."

Satisfied that Grandma and Grandpa were safely occupied purchasing food staples, colorful yard goods, and crinkly bright tissue paper, Hollis set out on a scouting mission to the back of the store. He found what he was looking for and edged toward the front of the store with it hidden behind him.

Grandma was looking at buttons. "Oh, Sanford, these are so lovely!" she exclaimed.

Seeing Hollis standing awkwardly nearby, Grandpa took Grandma's elbow and steered her toward the front counter. "Another day, Hazel. Let's pay for what we have and see if there's any mail for us."

Hollis waited until they had completed their business before taking his own purchase to the counter. Mr. Pasco wrapped it for him and counted a few coins into his hand, change for the price of the hide. Wide-eyed, Hollis put the money into his pocket and turned toward the door.

"Don't forget your glue!" the storekeeper said.

"Thanks, Mr. Pasco," Hollis said, going out to join his grandparents on the wagon.

Grandma was reading to Grandpa from a white sheet of paper, but when Hollis emerged from the store, she quickly stuffed it into her pocket. Hollis was too absorbed in his secret scheme to notice.

He launched his plan that very night after supper, holing up in his room. He left it only occasionally, to borrow wax, string, some rags and one of Grandma's heavy flatirons. Grandpa and Grandma exchanged bewildered glances at his strange requests, but told him where to find the items. He worked on his project for the next three nights until he was satisfied with the job he had done.

The next evening after an early supper, the family piled into Grandpa's sleigh and set out for the annual District Three Christmas pageant. The little schoolhouse was packed when they arrived. Proud parents were crammed together on the long benches and lined up three or four deep along the back wall. The front wall was screened by a curtain made of two long white bed sheets hung from a taut wire stretched across the room. Behind that curtain waited the tittering, nervous children, who had been memorizing and rehearsing recitations and songs for the past two weeks and were now convinced they wouldn't remember a word.

Miss Kenyon, wearing a shiny green dress with a crisp white collar and cuffs, stepped out from behind the curtain to welcome the parents and introduce the primary students who would open the program. Lila and Lulu Webster, Jean-Paul and Thérèse Centerbar rummaged their way through the curtains and lined up in front of it. Beginning hesitantly, but gaining confidence with each sing-song line, they recited:

Welcome, neighbors, one and all.
We're glad to see you here.
We hope you all enjoy our show
We wish you Christmas cheer!

The thunderous applause they received sent the youngsters scurrying to their parents' waiting laps, clearing the makeshift stage for the acts to follow. There were more recitations, songs and skits. The grand finale was an enactment of the nativity story by the oldest students. A hush fell over the crowd as the lanterns were dimmed and the white sheets were drawn back to reveal a small manger with a large yellow star suspended over it. The silence was broken by a small voice chirping, "I helped paint the star, Mama."

Nicholas, hidden behind the right-hand curtain, began to narrate the Bible story in solemn tones. "'And it came to pass in those days, that there went out a decree from Caesar Augustus...'" and when he got to the part about Mary and Joseph going to Bethlehem, Iva Wainwright (who else?) came out dressed as Mary, wrapped in a sheet that her mother had dyed blue. Iva was followed somewhat reluctantly by Tommy Webster, who was supposed to be Joseph. Nicholas continued on, reading flawlessly. When he read of the shepherds, three of the older girls emerged from behind the left curtain wearing robes made of pillow ticking and beards made of bunches of sheep's wool. At that sight amusement rippled through the onlookers, who temporarily forgot the solemnity of this scene. Nicholas carefully watched the actors and paced his reading to coincide with their actions. Next it was Hollis' turn. He and Leroy and Arnold Twiss were the wise men. In the darkness behind the left curtain they hurriedly made the final adjustments to their royal robes and crowns. Nicholas read, "'Now when Jesus was born in Bethlehem of Judaea in the days of Herod the king, behold, there came wise men from the East...'" The three had just begun to proceed from behind the curtain when Leroy exclaimed in a panic-struck stage whisper, "The gifts!"

In great disorder they lunged back behind the curtain to pick up the treasures they were to present to the baby Jesus. Somehow the audience managed to restrain themselves from laughing as the boys reappeared, crowns askew, bearing gifts. Leroy proudly held aloft a vinegar cruet bearing the label "FRANKINCENSE." Arnold carried an earthenware jug dubbed "MYRRH," while Hollis brought up the rear with a bowl full to overflowing with thin slices of a maple sapling, which the boys had painted yellow to look like gold coins. Evidently their efforts had achieved greater realism than they knew, for suddenly the silence was broken by Marie's all-too-audible voice saying, "Look, Papa! Hollis did find the gold!"

Hollis froze in mid-step. He could see Jock's face contorting as he struggled to keep himself from laughing. Grandma and Grandpa were having similar difficulty. He looked at Nicholas, hoping he would continue the narration to distract attention away from him, but Nicholas was doubled over with silent laughter, his hand clasped tightly over his mouth and tears streaming down his face. That was all Hollis could stand. Howls of hilarity erupted from him as he realized the silliness of the situation. Soon the whole school-house rocked with merriment.

Miss Kenyon quickly drew the curtains to allow the laughter to

Miss Kenyon

subside. She repositioned the actors, straightening robes, securing beards and balancing crowns. Before signaling Nicholas to begin, she turned to Hollis. "Are you all right now?" she asked with a twinkle.

He nodded, relieved that she was not angry. The curtains were opened and the play finished without further mishap. During the round of congratulations that followed, it was generally agreed (by everyone except Iva) that this had been the best Christmas pageant ever. Family by family, the little schoolhouse emptied out into the starlit night. All around could be heard the muffled sound of hoof-beats on the snowy road and the jingle of sleigh bells. As Grandpa guided Jackie and Gwen down Mill Creek Road, Hollis curled up contentedly in the thick blankets in the back of the sleigh. Savoring the scent of wood smoke in the crisp Adirondack night air, he reflected on the events of the evening. It had been, he thought, a nearly perfect night.

13

Christmas in Thurman

Hollis blinked his eyes. It was still dark, but he knew he had overslept. And any doubt he might have had was abruptly removed by the broomstick pounding on the ceiling.

"Are you going to sleep all day?" Grandpa shouted good-naturedly. "It's Christmas Eve and there's lots to be done!"

Hollis sprang from the bed. He had to be ready when Gibby arrived! Gibby was taking firewood to Warrensburg today, and had promised to pick up Hollis' present and deliver it to Ma, but Hollis had a better idea.

"Grandma," he said as soon as he reached the kitchen, "could I go to Warrensburg with Gibby today? That way I could give Ma her present in person."

A slight frown crossed Grandma's face. "Your ma will be working at the hotel, I'm sure. You probably wouldn't even get to see her. Besides, we don't even know if Gibby would want to take you this time."

"He promised he would take me some time," Hollis said is a pleading tone.

Grandma exchanged glances with Grandpa.

"Your grandma's right, son," said Grandpa. "And besides," he added, almost as an afterthought, "I'll need you to help me cut the Christmas tree."

117

"And then we'll have to decorate it!" Grandma chimed in cheerfully.

Knowing better than to argue, Hollis turned and went back upstairs, trying to hide the tears of disappointment that threatened to spill from his eyes. He returned to the kitchen with his mother's gift just as Gibby pulled into the yard. He heard the big man kicking the snow from his boots on the porch and opened the door to let him in.

"How's my partner doing today?" Gibby asked, clapping Hollis warmly on the shoulder.

Normally the sight of Gibby would make Hollis break out into a grin, but today he could only answer glumly, "Fine."

Gibby raised an eyebrow in surprise, but said nothing about Hollis' unusual demeanor.

"Gibby, sit and have coffee," Grandma instructed.

"Thank you, Hazel, I will. It'll be the last warm thing in this belly for hours, and it's going to be a cold ride today. Looks like we could get more snow before the day is out."

"I hope you don't have any trouble making it back tonight," Grandma said, casting a worried glance outside.

Gibby seemed unconcerned. "If the snow is too heavy, I'll stay the night at my cousin's and get an early start in the morning. In any event," he concluded, with a sly wink at Grandma, "I'll have that special item you ordered back here in time for your Christmas celebration."

"And you'll be sure to give my gift to Ma?" Hollis prompted.

For a second Gibby looked confused, and then quickly recovered. "To be sure, I will," he said, taking the package.

Hollis wondered what "special item" Grandma had asked Gibby to bring, but he didn't have long to think about it. As soon as Gibby was on his way, Grandma and Grandpa busied Hollis with an endless round of chores. All morning he was kept on the run with trips to the barn, trips to the storeroom and trips to the cellar.

After dinner he and Grandpa bundled up to brave the storm in search of a Christmas tree. Hollis carried the small saw while Grandpa devoted all his efforts to maintaining his balance in the snow. Slowly they made their way out past the barns and through the pasture to the row of trees that bordered it.

"Look here, Grandpa!" Hollis said, pointing out a young pine tree about six feet tall.

Grandpa eyed it critically. "Looks a little puny to me," he said. "Seems to me there were some good ones over by the orchard."

Hollis sighed a little impatiently, but followed Grandpa to the edge of the apple orchard. There they discussed the merits of several young evergreens they encountered. Each, according to Grandpa, had some flaw—too short, too tall, too thin, a bend in the trunk, or a hole in the foliage.

"Grandpa, look! This one's perfect!" Hollis cried as he spied a spruce tree off to one side.

They examined it closely and found it flawless. Under Grandpa's watchful eye, Hollis scooped the snow from around the base of the tree and sawed through its trunk.

By the time they had dragged it back to the barn, sawed the bottom flat, secured it to a stand constructed of crossed boards and carried it up to the porch, it was nearly dark, and there was still no sign of Gibby.

Grandma was ecstatic about the tree, admiring it from every angle. "Such a beautiful spruce!" she exclaimed. "Let's put it over in the corner."

They placed it where she instructed, only to be told, "No, I think over here more, in front of the window."

Dutifully, Hollis dragged the tree over in front of the window.

"No, no. It was better where it was!" Back went the tree and out came the box of tin candle holders. Grandpa carefully clipped the holders to the tree branches and outfitted each with a tiny candle. Grandma and Hollis added little bells to the tree and stepped back to admire the effect.

After supper the job of stringing popcorn fell to Hollis, and by the time that job was done it was time to turn in. Hollis took one more look out the window. The snow had let up a little, but there was no sign of Gibby's sleigh.

"More than likely he decided to spend the night in Warrensburg," Grandma said comfortingly. "He'll be here in the forenoon for sure, bringing a special Christmas treat. We'll have a good Christmas."

Hollis let the curtain drop back into place and turned toward the room. "I know. I was just hoping he'd get here. I wanted to know how Ma is, and what she said when he gave her my present. I was wondering—" Suddenly his disappointment threatened to make his voice crack, so he let his sentence trail off.

"Hollis, maybe I should tell—" Grandma began, when Grandpa cut her off.

"What your Grandma is saying is, maybe we should get you off to bed now, so you'll be bright-eyed and bushy-tailed in the morning. There's still chores in the morning, you know."

Hollis bade them goodnight and went up to his room. Near the stovepipe he caught a snatch of conversation from the kitchen below. The first voice was Grandma's. "San, maybe we should have told him. I can't bear—"

"He'll know soon enough, Hazel. It's better like this, in case something goes wrong."

Hollis drifted off to sleep, wondering what it was that his grandparents were keeping from him and what it was that could go wrong, but when he awoke he had forgotten all about it. The scent of hot coffee and sizzling bacon filled the house, and he leapt out of bed to get dressed.

"You'd better get down here before your grandfather eats all the buckwheat cakes!" Grandma warned.

Hollis needed no more urging, but raced down to take his place at the table. A mountain of the cakes awaited him and he ate until he could barely move. From where he was seated he could see some intriguing bundles under the tree.

"Well," Grandpa said after his second cup of coffee, "I guess the stock would like to have Christmas breakfast, too. Are you coming, boy," he added with a playful poke at Hollis, "or are you going to sit here and eat all day?"

"Coming!" Hollis managed to answer with his mouth still full, and together they bundled up and went to the barn. Hollis led the way with the shovel, clearing a track for Grandpa to walk.

They took their time with the chores. Hollis threw down hay for the horses, cows and sheep while Grandpa milked, and then cleaned out the pens and shoveled the path to the creek while Grandpa spread fresh hay around. They collected what eggs there were and returned to the house, Hollis again shoveling to widen the path.

It was then that Hollis decided to broach the subject of making syrup. Gathering up all his courage, he cleared his throat and said, "Grandpa, I've been thinking, and I've got a great idea!"

Grandpa set down the pail of milk and the basket of eggs and paused, catching his breath. "What's your idea?" he asked with a smile.

"Well, I've been thinking about the—" he hesitated, suddenly worried about bringing up the subject that had caused Grandpa so much sadness. He started again. "Well, you know, I was out walking on the other side of the pond, and I came across the..." He paused, stuck again.

Grandpa tensed slightly as he said, "You found the sugarhouse?"

It was now or never. Hollis plunged in. "Yes, the sugarhouse. And it's just sitting there, doing nothing. And I thought, I mean, I wondered—couldn't we make syrup there, you and me? You could teach me how to make the syrup to sell in Saratoga Springs? I mean, if you thought it would be all right." Suddenly out of steam, he let his voice trail off. He must have been crazy to think that Grandpa would agree to this.

Grandpa was silent.

Hollis thought of all the arguments he had prepared to convince Grandpa, how he would say that he was a hard worker, and how he would remind Grandpa how much stronger he had gotten. But how could he argue with silence?

He waited, practically holding his breath. Still Grandpa said nothing. He tried to guess what Grandpa was thinking by looking at his face, but his features were a mask. Finally, without saying a word, Grandpa picked up the pail and basket and proceeded toward the house. Hollis, totally frustrated, followed along with the shovel. Apparently the subject was closed. They returned to the house as though nothing had happened.

He and Grandpa had just washed up and put on fresh shirts when they heard the sound of Gibby's rig in the yard.

"Why don't you go out and see what he's brought?" Grandma said, twinkling.

Forgetting for the moment about the failed maple syrup conversation, Hollis raced out the door, leaving Grandma and Grandpa in the doorway. He stopped suddenly, for Gibby was not alone. A small figure bundled up in carriage robes and scarves was seated beside him. Hollis waited while Gibby lifted his passenger to the ground, then started forward slowly. The figure turned, and robes and scarves suddenly went flying every which way.

"Hollis!"

Hollis couldn't believe his eyes. "Ma!" he cried, running to meet her.

Ma hugged him till he could hardly breathe, tears brimming in her eyes. "You're a sight for sore eyes!" she said. "I swear you've grown two inches. It must be your Grandma's good cooking." She turned then to the Ingrahams. "Merry Christmas!"

"Merry Christmas," Grandma said, smiling broadly.

Grandpa just nodded.

Grandma took charge. "Come in, Mary, come in. Don't you boys stand out there and freeze. Come in," she added, herding them through the doorway.

Gibby promised he'd be in as soon as he unloaded Ma's things from his sleigh. A few minutes later he joined them in the kitchen. He placed Ma's bags on the floor and turned to Grandma. "I have to go, Hazel. My folks are waiting Christmas on me."

Grandma gave him a hug. "Of course you must go. Thank you for helping us with our surprise."

"Yeah, thanks, Gibby!" Hollis chimed in enthusiastically.

"I was glad to do it," he replied, turning to go. "Say, Hollis," he said as an afterthought, reaching into his coat and withdrawing the package Hollis had wrapped for Ma. "I thought you'd like to give this to your Ma yourself." He climbed aboard his wagon. "Merry Christmas, San, Hazel! Merry Christmas, Hollis!" In a softer voice he added, "Mary, I took care of that little matter we discussed. Merry Christmas." He snapped his whip over the oxen and was headed on down the lane.

"Well, now," said Grandpa, "it looks as if someone here is ready for Christmas. What do you say, Mother? Have we waited long enough? And shall we light the tree now or wait until it gets dark?"

They decided to delay the lighting of the tiny candles, but to exchange gifts right away. Hollis raced upstairs and pulled a burlap bag from under his bed. Cradling it in his arms, he returned to the kitchen, and sat down, carefully placing the sack at his feet. He began by giving his gift to his mother. Ma exclaimed over the wrapping job and undid the paper with exasperating slowness. "Oh," she exclaimed, "this is beautiful!"

Her fingers traced the design etched on the fungus. "Crane Mountain! How many times I have pictured this in my mind. Now I can look at it any time I want and think of you here." She gave Hollis a hug. "And the Bible verse is perfect. 'I will lift up mine eyes unto the hills.' Thank you, son."

Pleased, but embarrassed, Hollis reached into the burlap bag and pulled out a bulky item tied up in a blue-flowered flour sack. He handed it to Grandma, saying, "Here, Grandma. Grandpa and I made this for you. Open it!"

Grandma looked surprised as she took it. "For me?" she asked, hurriedly unknotting the yarn that tied it. Out of the sack she pulled a foot-long wooden board with a V-shaped notch cut in one end. She immediately placed it on the floor. A brace near the notch held that end up off the surface. "You made me a boot jack!" Grandma said with obvious pleasure. "I hope this means—" she paused to direct meaningful looks at Hollis and Grandpa— "that there will be more boots lined up on the porch and fewer dirty boots tracking across my clean floors from now on!"

"Yes, ma'am," Hollis said with a grin. "Yes, ma'am," said his partner in crime, winking at Hollis. Grandpa was definitely getting into the holiday spirit.

Next it was Grandma's turn to distribute gifts. She had made Grandpa a fine new pair of brown buff mittens, much heavier than regular knitted mittens. They reminded Hollis of the hooked rug his mother had had at home. For Ma there was a thick knitted muffler of brown and white nubby yarn, a gift from Grandma and Grandpa. Ma immediately wrapped it around her neck and chin, tossing one long tasseled end over her shoulder. Her eyes sparkled with pleasure. "Oh, Mother Ingraham, it's so thick! It will keep me toasty warm on cold days!"

"Let me see," Grandma said, inspecting Ma as she turned this way and that. "It looks just fine. Goes good with your coloring, too."

Grandma then turned to Hollis. "Now for you, young man." Out from under the tree she pulled a bulky package, which she presented to him.

Tearing open the wrapper he discovered a lovingly-stitched pair of woolen trousers, just like those worn by the men on the hunting expedition. "Gee, Grandma, thanks!" he exclaimed, holding them up. "These are great, and they're the same kind of wool as Grandpa's old coat in the storeroom."

"Grandpa's old coat that used to be in the storeroom," she corrected him with a twinkle, letting him realize that she had remodeled the coat into these trousers. "Now you'll be all set for cold weather. I made them good and big, hoping they'll do for next winter, too."

"How will we keep him from growing?" Ma asked, laughing.

"We'll have to set one of Mother's flat irons on his head," Grandpa joked, speaking to her for the first time.

"Well," said Ma a little more seriously, "I guess we're going to have to let him grow up a little bit. She took a small package from her bag and handed it to Hollis. "I think you're old enough to have this now," she said, smiling.

Hollis' eyes widened in amazement when he ripped open the paper and discovered the most beautiful folding penknife he had ever seen. It had a bone handle and two shiny blades that folded in and out with ease. "Just as smooth as butter," he exclaimed, hugging his mother and displaying the knife to his grandparents. "My own knife! This is the best present ever!"

"I think he likes it," Ma said, laughing. "Father Ingraham, would you teach him to use it safely?"

Grandpa nodded approvingly. "A boy his age should have a knife. Should know how to use it safely, too. I'll teach him."

"Father Ingraham," began Ma. She hesitantly, "I have a gift for you, too."

"A gift for me?" Grandpa said. Hollis thought he sounded embarrassed. "You shouldn't be spending money on gifts for me."

"I didn't," Ma said. Her voice softened a bit as she continued. "It's something Johnny sent away for just before the accident. I forgot all about it, what with all that happened. It was Gibby who reminded me, just recently. It came in at the depot after the tannery fire, and Gibby picked it up and has had it stored away all this time."

Hollis was mystified. Ma was empty-handed. "Where is it, Ma?"

Her answer was directed to Grandpa rather than to him. "Gibby left it out on the side porch for you. Come, let's go open it." As if to reinforce the invitation, she took his coat from its hook and wrapped it snugly around Grandpa's shoulders. She took his arm to help him from his chair and said gently, "Come, we'll go together."

Hollis wanted to rush out to the porch to see the mystery package that his father had bought so long ago, but he sensed there was a lot more going on than a simple gift exchange. He and Grandma hung back and trailed behind Ma and Grandpa. Out on the porch they formed a semicircle around two large wooden crates leaning against the house. Gibby had left a pry bar beside them.

Grandpa stood silently looking at the crates.

"Open them, Grandpa," Hollis urged, dying of curiosity.

Without further ado, Grandpa picked up the bar and began to pry the lid off the nearest crate. It was half off before he realized what was nestled in the excelsior-lined box. He almost stumbled backward as his eyes took in the shiny metal contents.

"What is it?" Hollis asked.

Grandpa's voice was softer than he had ever heard it before, and it sounded as though he was talking to himself. "It's the evaporating pans. He did it. Johnny bought the evaporating pans."

Grandpa looked at Ma, and he groped for words to express his feelings. "I never knew," he said. "I never guessed what he was doing, why he left to go to the tannery. I thought...Mary, I...." He stopped speaking, unable to continue.

Ma came to his rescue, saying gently. "I know. I understand. No need to say anymore. How could you have known? I was so upset,

I never told you." She paused a minute, then said in a matter-of-fact voice, "There are lots of metal buckets, too. Gibby says he'll bring them down next time he comes."

Grandpa took out his handkerchief and blew his nose loudly. Grandma quickly took charge. "Let's get in out of this cold!"

They all trooped back inside, glad for the warmth of the shiny black stove.

Ma smiled and took a prettily wrapped package to Grandma. Grandma exclaimed over the wrapping, which she carefully removed and folded. Only then did she look at the gift itself, a lace-edged handkerchief with violets embroidered in one corner. Grandma was obviously moved. "I'll treasure this," she said. "No one does tatting and embroidery like you, Mary."

Ma demurred, "It's just a little something I do to busy my hands in the evenings. I did the violets because I remembered how partial you are to the spring wildflowers, always keeping a bouquet of them on your table."

"I'll take it to church with me," Grandma exclaimed.

Grandpa shook his head. "All this fuss over a hanky. Hollis, help me up. We need to go out to the barn."

Hollis supported Grandpa as he shifted his weight to his feet. Grandma looked at the clock on the shelf. "Kind of early for chores, isn't it?" she asked.

"You never mind that," Grandpa said. "You ladies just go on talking about hankies and recipes and such, and we men will be right back. This time I have a surprise!" Mystified, Hollis put on his coat and followed Grandpa to the barn. He had never seen Grandpa in such good spirits. It was hard to believe that this was the same man who had refused to talk to him earlier that day. Even the sharp lines in his face seemed to have softened.

Once they were in the barn Grandpa headed straight to the loft ladder. "I have a present for you, but I need your young legs to fetch it down for me," he said. "Climb halfway up that ladder."

Hollis did as he was told.

Grandpa pointed to what appeared to be a board that was held up under the ceiling rafters by two strips of wood tacked to the rafters on either side. Concealed by cobwebs and dust, it had never caught his attention before. This was a present? "Now slide it off those strips of wood and hand it down to me," Grandpa said.

Balancing precariously on the step of the loft ladder, Hollis managed to push the board until one end tipped down to where Grandpa could reach it and pull it the rest of the way down. He scrambled down to see what it was. His grandfather had begun rubbing the dust off it with a feed sack. He handed the sack to Hollis. Gesturing toward the dirty board he said, "This is for you. Why don't you clean it off?"

Hollis rubbed with the coarse burlap, reading the carved letters revealed as the accumulated grime of years disappeared. "'I'-'n'-'g'," he read as he rubbed. He began to polish faster then, as the realization of what was there began to dawn on him. At last it was all cleaned off, and Hollis could hardly believe what he saw. "Ingraham & Ingraham, Pure Maple Syrup," the sign said.

"If we're going to go into business together," Grandpa said, "we'd better put up a sign."

"You mean it?" Hollis squealed excitedly. "We can do it? We can make syrup?"

"We can, but don't think it will be easy," Grandpa cautioned. "It'll be hard work, and with my bad leg, I can only help you with part of it."

"I have two good legs, and I don't mind hard work," Hollis exclaimed eagerly.

"I know that, or I wouldn't even be considering it. But you've got to know, when the sap is flowing, there won't be time for anything but sugaring. You'll be so tired you could fall asleep standing on your feet. And when you finally get time to lie down and rest, every bone in your body will ache."

"I don't care!" Hollis said happily.

"I can teach you when and how to tap the trees." Grandpa stroked his beard. "And I can boil the sap down to syrup while you're collecting it. We'll make a good team, you and me," Grandpa said with a warm smile, as they started back to the house, with Hollis hugging the sign close to his chest. "Of course, we're going to have to figure out how to use those newfangled evaporating pans," he chuckled.

When they arrived at the house, Hollis proudly showed off the sign for the sugarhouse. Ma and Grandma were speechless at first, and then they couldn't stop talking, exclaiming over and over again how wonderful it would be to have Ingraham & Ingraham back in production again. As the excitement slowly subsided, Hollis suddenly remembered his own wonderful Christmas scheme.

"Grandpa!" he said excitedly.

"Yes?"

"I-I have something for you, too. I hope you like it." He pulled from the burlap bag under his feet, something in a flour sack tied up with a piece of string and put it on Grandpa's lap. Grandpa looked questioningly at Grandma, who shrugged her shoulders and shook her head as if to say she knew nothing about it.

As soon as he put his hand on the gift, Grandpa could tell what was inside the sack. He struggled to control his emotions, but his hand had a tell-tale tremor as he fumbled with the tie. After what seemed like an eternity to the intrigued onlookers, he reached into the sack and withdrew a fiddle, his own fiddle, painstakingly glued back together and polished to a mirror-like shine. Grandpa said nothing. He ran his hands over the fiddle, stroking its familiar curves and delicately arched top, plucking idly at the strings. It was impossible to read the emotions in his lined face

Hollis didn't know what to say, so he kept still. Ma put her hand comfortingly on his arm.

It was Grandma who broke the uncomfortable silence. Dabbing at her eyes with the corner of her apron, she said briskly, "I think we ought to light the tree! We don't need to wait until it's dark. Hollis, get me the matches." Hollis handed a box of wooden kitchen matches to her, and she carefully lighted each tiny candle until the little spruce tree glowed..

For a moment they watched the tree in a breathless hush.

Then the silence was broken by the rasping of a bow being drawn softly across the strings of a violin. Haltingly at first, and then becoming stronger and surer, a melody began to swell from Grandpa's fiddle.

As if in support, Grandma's voice joined in, followed by the voices of Hollis and Ma:

The Fiddle

What Child is this, who, laid to rest,
On Mary's lap is sleeping?
Whom angels greet with anthems sweet,
While shepherds watch are keeping?
This, this is Christ the King,
Whom shepherds guard and angels sing:
Haste, haste to bring Him laud,
The Babe, the Son of Mary.

The candles on the little spruce tree were burning low as the last plaintive note faded away. Wordlessly Grandma extinguished them, one by one. The last light flickered and then was gone, but the glow of that Christmas would linger in all their hearts forever.

14

Planning

Ma stayed for six days. Hollis excitedly introduced her to the livestock, and showed off his expertise at doing chores. Hollis and his mother took long walks around the snowy farm and talked and talked. They talked about her job working for Mrs. Emerson at the hotel, and how she had been able to begin paying off their bills. She enjoyed meeting the interesting guests at the hotel, and liked Mrs. Emerson, who, she said, was a fair taskmaster and a kind person. It had been Mrs. Emerson who had suggested that, since the hotel was not too busy over the holiday, she should take some time to visit her son. They talked about school and about his new friends.

One day Hollis took her to the sugarhouse. He wasn't sure how she would feel about seeing it again, but once inside, he could see that it brought back happy memories for her. Suddenly she was talking about the days when she, Johnny, Grandpa, Gibby and Grandma had worked the sugaring season there. She spoke of his father, of his love for sugaring and his excitement about improving and expanding the maple operation. She pointed to the stone box-like structure in the center of the sugarhouse. "This was to be the firebox to support the evaporating pans. He read all about how to build it and operate it to get the best possible fire. That way he could boil the first run sap quickly and keep the delicate flavor of the syrup. He spent a lot of time working on this the summer before he died, hauling these stones in and laying them up."

"He and Grandpa could have earned a lot more money by making the syrup the modern way?"

Ma arched her eyebrows in surprise. "Yes, I guess so," she said, "but it was never about the money. It was about doing a better job. It was about making better syrup. With the evaporating pans, your pa and grandpa could have made pure light syrup, and that was what excited him so. He took great pride and satisfaction in doing the best job he could."

Hollis thought about that a bit. A few months earlier he might not have understood that idea, but now he thought about the pleasure he felt when he did his chores well, when the animals were happily munching their hay, swishing their well-groomed tails in clean pens that were carefully lined with fresh bedding. He knew that kind of satisfaction. Still, there were more questions.

"But, Ma, wasn't it earning money for the evaporating pans that got Pa—" he hesitated, then said it, "killed?"

"No," Ma said firmly. "I've had time to think about it. It was an accident that caused your pa's death. He died trying to pull another man out of a fire. It could have happened anytime, anywhere, because life is like that. Death comes to all of us, some early, some late. It was just very hard for me to accept that he was gone from us so soon."

"Why didn't you ever talk to me about it?"

Ma shook her head. "I don't know. At first you were too young, and I was too upset. Then, as time went by, it just seemed better to keep it to myself. I couldn't see anything to be gained by bringing it up. I didn't realize that you needed to know."

She walked around the sugarhouse then, touching the familiar buckets and kettles, and finally turned to him. "And now you are a young man, and you will pick up where your father left off. It will be a fine thing to see you sugaring with your grandfather."

Christmas week flew by. There were the usual tasks to be done, but there was an extra pair of hands to help. Never one to be idle, Ma helped Grandma with jobs around the house. Together they spent their days baking, cooking, washing up the dishes, sweeping, and doing the washing and ironing. In the evenings they cut out and sewed new aprons or did mending or knitting by the stove. Grandma seemed to love having a woman around to visit with. Gibby came down three times that week. Three times! Hollis could barely believe it.

First he came down to bring the new sap buckets. He joined the family for a cup of coffee at the table, lingering over it to visit awhile. Hollis told him excitedly about the plan to reopen the sugarhouse that spring, and proudly showed off the sign Grandpa had given him.

"Sanford," Gibby said to Grandpa, "you know my offer to help is still open. I can drive the sled with the collecting vat on it, and help the boy carry buckets to it. It'd be like old times to be part of the Ingraham and Ingraham team again."

Grandpa nodded. "We'd be obliged. The boy's a good worker, but he won't be able to handle it alone. Maybe the Centerbar boy could help out, too. He looks like a decent sort. If it's a good run this year, it will take a lot of hands, and we could use him." They continued talking, and Hollis was drawn into the magic of the plan to turn sap into syrup.

But first there were the buckets to deal with. Gibby and Grandpa decided that it made the most sense to put the buckets and sap pans right in the sugarhouse, so Hollis climbed aboard his sleigh to help take them over. As an afterthought, he went and got his sign and added it to the load.

They couldn't take the shortcut around the pond because there was no way across the creek that way. They would have to use the old roadway that left the farm lane on the other side of the bridge. He and Gibby loaded the evaporating pans onto the sleigh with the buckets and started out.

They went out the lane to the place where the sugarhouse road forked off it. "I don't think the oxen can pull the sleigh through there without us breaking a trail first," Gibby said to Hollis after looking the situation over carefully. He unhitched the animals from the wagon and, walking behind them with the reins twitching over their backs, coaxed and whistled to them to urge them forward. Hollis walked beside him. "Come closer to sugaring, we'll need to break trails all through the sugar bush to get the sap down to the sugarhouse."

It was slow going through the deep snow, but eventually the sugarhouse loomed into sight. Gibby circled the oxen so they were facing back out, and they retraced their steps. The going was easier this time, as the grade was downhill and some of the snow had been knocked down by their first pass through it. When they reached the farm lane Gibby decided the trail was good enough for the oxen to drag the sled, so he hitched them up and successfully drove in to the sugarhouse.

Hollis unlatched the sugarhouse door and propped it open wide, then grabbed an end of the first evaporator pan crate and helped carry it inside. After carrying the second one, they took in the new buckets and stacked them with the others and leaned the sign up in the corner. Gibby put his hands on his hips and looked around. "The place looks good. I haven't been in here since the spring before your Pa died."

Hollis lifted the lid off of one of the shipping crates. Some pieces of paper fluttered in the breeze that blew through the door, and he pulled them out. "Look," he said excitedly, "here are instructions on how to set up the pans!"

"Take those back to the house with you. They'll be a help to you and your Grandpa." When they returned to the farm lane, Hollis climbed down to walk back to the house while Gibby left for home.

The next time Gibby came back, it was to have dinner with them. When Hollis opened the door for him, he was surprised to see him with his hair all slicked down and a freshly-ironed shirt buttoned all the way up to his chin. Hollis almost asked him why he was so dressed up, but just then Ma came over to the door to greet Gibby and take his coat. The two of them started talking and laughing, and there was no time for asking questions or even getting a word in edgewise all the way through supper. Hollis realized that, for the first time, Ma had begun to look like the girl in the photograph.

After supper Ma helped Grandma wash up, and Hollis, Gibby and Grandpa talked some more about sugaring. When Ma and Grandma joined them beside the stove Grandpa got out his fiddle and tuned it up. Gibby beamed with pleasure as Grandpa played a dreamy-sounding waltz followed by a lively jig.

"I'm rusty," Grandpa said apologetically. "It'll take my fingers awhile to get back in shape to do those fast ones again!" He carefully placed the fiddle on the clock shelf. "Hollis, why don't you run get some popping corn for us to pop over the fire?"

Hollis ran up to the storeroom to get some of the corn for Grandpa to put in the popper, and Grandma brought some apples up from the cellar. The corn kernels made soft explosions as they turned into fluffy white morsels in the wire popping basket that Grandpa shook over the stove, and the smell was irresistible. Grandma poured the popped corn into a large bowl and stirred in a dollop of fresh butter and some salt. They enjoyed their treats beside the big iron stove until Gibby announced reluctantly that it was time for him to go home, as he would need to get up extra early the next morning.

And the next morning was Gibby's last visit with them that week. He had come to pick up Ma to take her back to Warrensburg. Hollis had known the day was coming when Ma would have to leave, but he had pushed the thought from his mind, as though wishing would make it not so. He was not alone in his misery that day. Grandma looked sad, and even Grandpa seemed reluctant to let her go. Gibby, for his part, looked as dejected as Hollis felt. "It won't be forever," Ma reassured Hollis as she hugged him for the last time before climbing onto Gibby's bobsleigh. It was still dark when they pulled out of the yard for the long trip, after many hugs and "thank yous" and promises to write.

"Come on, boy," Grandpa said with a sigh, "the stock's waiting for us."

The rest of that day Hollis had a hard time settling into any of the activities that he normally enjoyed around the house. Finally Grandma, after watching him wandering aimlessly around the kitchen, suggested he go hunt up his friends and see if anybody wanted to go sledding. "French Hill is too steep and dangerous, but the hill on Mill Creek Road above Tom Webster's is a great one. There's an old toboggan hanging in the barn that used to belong to your Pa. Why don't you take it along? Just be back by dark to help your Grandpa with chores."

Hollis found the toboggan and pulled it out the lane to French Hill. He decided to stick it into a snow bank and hike up to the Centerbar house. Maybe they would go sledding. Anyway, he was dying to talk to Nicholas about the plans for sugaring and ask him if he would help. He had barely begun the climb up the hill when he heard the voices and laughter of the Centerbar children on their way down. As they rounded the curve in the road, Hollis could see that Nicholas was carrying a makeshift sled made from a piece of roofing metal. Someone had carefully folded all the sharp edges under and curved up the front end.

"It's Hollis!" Marie shouted excitedly, and all the children

Grandma and Grandpa

called out a greeting and talked about the fun they would have sliding down the hill by the Websters' house. It was a wonderful day for it. The snow on the road was packed hard from sleigh runners traveling over it. The occasional sleigh that might travel the road that day would not endanger the children, as they would have plenty of time to get out of its way. Besides, everybody who used the road would be wary, expecting youngsters to be out sledding on that hill on a day like this. Hollis loaded the three youngest Centerbars on his toboggan, and he and Nicholas took turns pulling it until they reached the top of Webster's hill.

Even before they got there they could hear the shrieks of excitement from the Webster children, who were already zipping down the hill on a variety of contrivances. The smallest children took turns riding in an oversized dishpan, which had handles on either side to hold onto. They twirled around crazily in their downhill descent. A couple of the older girls used a sheet of roofing metal like Nicholas, and Tommy had a homemade skipjack. On the bottom it had a single runner that appeared to have been made from a barrel stave, and it had a hip-high seat perched on a post that stood up in the middle. Hollis watched him carefully balance himself on the seat as the skipjack raced down the hill into the hollow and continued up the other side, almost climbing to the top. It was a teetery ride, but he made it. Tommy gave a whoop and triumphantly raised his arms above his head. "Come on! We'll wait on this side until you come over," he shouted to the others. "It's slicker'n all get out, so hold on good!"

Hollis climbed aboard the toboggan with the youngest Centerbar children. He didn't say so, but he was worried that they might be cut on the roofing metal sled if they slid into a snow bank. Nicholas would take the older kids on that and try to keep them safe.

Tommy was right. The hill was slick and the sledding was exciting. They made run after run, until it grew late. It was Nicholas who finally made the first move to end the fun. "Come on, we've got to go home. It's going to be dark soon, and the little ones are getting cold."

Hollis and the Centerbars trudged back toward French Hill. It was then that Hollis told Nicholas about all the exciting events of Christmas and the new plan to sugar when the thaw came. "And Grandpa said we'd be needing extra help, and you could work with us if you wanted!" he concluded excitedly.

"Really? Me?" Nicholas asked.

Hollis repeated what Grandpa had said about him, and Nicholas glowed with the compliment. He passed along to his friend the warning about how difficult the work would be. Nicholas, as he had expected, was not afraid of the idea of hard work. They parted company at the turnoff to the farm, and Hollis hurried on to help with chores. Before supper Grandma told him to bring extra firewood. "It's turning bitter," she said. "We'll have to keep the fire hot all night."

She was right. Sunday was bitter, and Monday was worse. Wind was rattling the windows when Hollis awoke. His nose was almost frozen, and crawling out from under his covers was the last thing he wanted to do.

He could hear Grandma downstairs stoking the fire. Reluctantly he swung his feet over the side of the bed, yelping as they hit the icy floor. He scrambled out of his nightshirt and into his barn clothes as quickly as possible and went to the washstand to splash water on his face. To his surprise, when he tipped the pitcher to pour water into the bowl, nothing came out; a layer of ice had sealed it inside.

He scooted down the steps two at a time, eager to huddle by the stove for a few minutes before he would have to thrust himself outside to do the barn chores. Grandpa was pulling on his boots. "It's a cold one today," he said, as though Hollis didn't already know it.

"You two bundle up," Grandma warned. "I'll have a good hot breakfast for you when you get back."

The sharp wind sliced through their clothing as they made their way to the barn, and Hollis tried to draw his head down into his coat, turtle fashion. He did his chores faster than he had ever done them before, even though he had the additional task of taking the ax down to the creek and chopping a hole in the ice for the stock to drink. There were only four eggs to carry back to the house with the milk that morning. Hollis wanted to race up the path and back to the warmth of the stove, but forced himself to match his pace to Grandpa's.

Once they were back at the porch water pump, Grandpa pulled off the heavy old rugs Grandma had draped over it the night before. "Sure hope it's not froze up!" he said. He worked the pump handle up and down. A smile creased his face as sparkling water flowed out the spout and into the enamel washbasin. He replaced the rugs, and Hollis carried the basin indoors and set it on the stove to warm for a few minutes before they attempted to clean up.

After breakfast Hollis layered up all the clothes he could comfortably wear and started off for school. At the end of the lane he met the Centerbars. Jean-Paul, Marie and Thérèse were buried in soft, furry deer hides on the sheet metal sled, which Nicholas was towing with a piece of braided rawhide. He and Hollis traded off pulling. It was a long walk to school that day.

The bitter cold clutched the mountains for nearly two weeks. Chore-times were painful, and the walk to and from school was brutal. Hollis came to love sitting by the stove in the evening. As soon as his schoolwork was finished, he and Grandpa would talk about sugaring.

"It will never be warm enough to start sugaring!" Hollis declared impatiently one evening.

"It won't be long now," Grandpa said. "When this cold eases up, there's lots we can do to start getting ready. We'll need to break open the roads through the sugar bush to get the sled through with the buckets and spouts. And we'll need to get that new equipment washed and set up."

For the hundredth time, Hollis went to the clock shelf, took down the instruction pages that had come with the evaporating pans, and he and Grandpa pored over them again, studying the diagrams. They saw the stone firebox, or "arch" as the directions called it, the arrangement of pans, pipes and spigots, and read how they worked. Grandpa shook his head in disbelief. "It sounds too good to be true," he said. "It says it boils the sap down faster, so you get more syrup using less firewood, and still it's good, light syrup. I hope it works!"

Each day it seemed the sun grew a little stronger and the air a

little warmer. Two weeks later, on a Saturday, Gibby brought his
oxen down so that he and Hollis could begin breaking trails. There
had been numerous snowfalls since Christmas, so even the road
from the lane to the sugarhouse needed to be done again. Grandpa
harnessed up Jackie and Gwen. Instead of hitching up the bobsleigh, he hooked up behind them a much smaller, lower sled-like
contraption. "We'll take the stone-boat," he said. "Jackie and Gwen
can get through with this after the oxen break the crust and help
pack down the road."

"Sanford," scolded Grandma, "don't you kill yourself falling off
that stone-boat and come complaining to me!"

Grandpa laughed, boarded the little sled and headed out the lane
behind Gibby and Hollis. They spent the entire morning laboriously urging the oxen and horses to wallow up and down the snow-
choked roads of the sugar bush. By noon they had a small network
of trails through the maple trees. "Why do we need so many
roads?" Hollis asked, surveying the work that they had done.

Gibby and Grandpa laughed. "You and young Centerbar will
wish we had more when you're carrying buckets of sap on snowshoes," Grandpa said. "The roads help get the sled with the gathering vat on it close to the trees, to save you steps and get the sap to
the sugarhouse faster."

They returned to the farmhouse to eat dinner and discuss a plan
for the afternoon. It might be weeks before sugaring season began,
but Grandpa thought they should go ahead and make use of the
newly broken roadways to begin getting the tapping equipment out
to the trees. "I've got a feeling it won't be long, now. It won't hurt
to get an early start. Let's take the buckets out and spread them out
through the sugarbush. That way, when the sap begins to flow, we'll
be able to get them up faster and we'll be able to start boiling sooner. The knowledge that Nicholas was planning to join the party for
the afternoon cemented the plan.

Nicholas was waiting for them at the sugarhouse, snowshoes in
hand, when they returned from the house. "I can see you were
thinking," Grandpa said, nodding approvingly at the snowshoes.
They set to work loading up the box of Gibby's bobsleigh with
stacks of metal buckets and lids. Grandpa took over the reins, and

Hollis, Nicholas and Gibby followed behind on snowshoes. Maneuvering the cumbersome snowshoes up the snowy trail was exhausting work for Hollis, and he had to struggle to keep up with Nicholas and Gibby, who were experienced in wearing them and moved along quite briskly. Every so often Grandpa would halt the oxen and Gibby and the boys would take a stack of buckets off the sled and place them upside down neatly beside the road. By the end of the day, all of the metal buckets except the new ones had been distributed through the sugarbush.

The next afternoon Hollis and Grandpa went back to the sugar-house to wash the new equipment. Hollis would need to carry water up from the pond. Grandpa pulled a long curved wooden contraption out of one corner and dusted it off with a cloth. He called it a yoke, and showed Hollis how to let it rest across his shoulders, with his neck nestled into a carved-out place in the middle. From each end hung a rope with a hook on it, and from each hook Grandpa suspended a bucket by its wire handle. "This will make it easier to carry the buckets," he said. "You'll need to make a couple of trips."

Hollis was pleased to discover that the yoke made the carrying much easier, which he especially appreciated because he had to carry the water uphill. By the time he returned with the first two buckets, Grandpa had started a fire in the woodstove and had pried the lids off of the crates. He had Hollis pour the water from his buckets into one of the enameled pots and place it on the stove to heat before returning to the pond with the empty pails. Grandpa met him at the sugarhouse door when he approached. "Come see this!" he said excitedly.

He ushered Hollis through the door, taking the filled buckets from his yoke. Hollis stared in wonderment. Grandpa had placed the evaporator pans on top of the arch and connected them. "Look," he said proudly, "see how perfectly they fit into the little ledge on top of the firebox. Johnny did a bang-up job!" Hollis admired the way the shallow box-like pans fit side by side across the top of the arch. They were carefully constructed of shiny tin, their seams neatly sealed with solder.

He poured the hot water from the pot on the stove into a galvanized tub and instructed Hollis to pour the second batch of water into the now empty pot and set it back on the stove to heat. He began to wash the new galvanized metal buckets.

"Where's the soap?" Hollis asked.

"No soap for this job," Grandpa said. "It gives the syrup an 'off' flavor, so we just use scalding hot water.

By the time the last bucket was scrubbed to Grandpa's satisfaction, the second pot of water had come to a boil. Grandpa poured a little into the evaporator pans and began giving it a going-over. While he did that, Hollis began carrying the washed buckets outside. He stacked them one by one upside down, making a large pyramid, so they could drain.

As they worked Grandpa told him the secrets of making quality syrup. "Cleanliness," he said. "It's all about keeping everything clean. You don't want bark and dirt and bugs to get into your sap, even though you're going to strain it later. And most of all, you don't want the sap to sour. To keep it from souring, you gotta keep things clean, and you gotta collect the sap often and boil it down right away. That's why I'm saving those wooden buckets for last. If we don't have to use them, I won't. They're hard to handle, and if sap sours in them, they are the dickens to clean out. If you don't clean 'em really good, the bucket sours the next batch of sap."

"Why do you keep them?" Hollis asked.

"Well, like I say, we might need them to tap all the trees fully. And they do keep the sap cooler on a warm day when the sap is flowing, but they're heavy, and they require preparation."

"What kind of preparation?"

"Well, when they are stored, the wood slats that make up the bucket dry out and shrink up. That makes the buckets leak, and it also means that when you turn the bucket upright, the hoops around them drop off. To prepare them we'd have to take them down to the pond and soak them till the wood swells up enough to close the cracks and hold the hoops in place. We'll see how it goes with Gibby and Nicholas next time they come. If we can make do with the galvanized pails, we will."

Together they carried the dry new buckets into the sugarhouse, stacking them neatly for their trip to the sugarbush. Grandpa and Hollis prepared to close up the sugarhouse. Suddenly Grandpa stopped. "The sign!" he said.

"What?" Hollis asked.

"We have to hang up the sign!" Grandpa retrieved the sign from the corner of the sugarhouse and nailed it neatly to the side of the sugarhouse beside the door. "Ingraham & Ingraham, Pure Maple Syrup," it proclaimed. They stepped back to admire it, then turned for home.

The preparations had been made. There was nothing to do but wait.

The Sign

15

Sugaring

The waiting ended a few days later with a single loud "plunk." Then another. And another, and another, and another. Soon the racing droplets of melting snow dropping off the house roof and hammering down onto the metal porch roof created such a racket that even Hollis was unable to sleep through it. He rolled over and rubbed his eyes, his sleepy brain trying to figure out what the strange noise was. Sudden understanding made him leap from his bed and throw open the window. It was not yet light out, but the moist rich air that greeted his nostrils signaled a definite change in the weather. He raced downstairs in his nightshirt and bare feet, shouting all the way. "Grandpa! Grandpa! It's here! Sugaring time is here!"

"So I hear," said Grandpa, emerging from his bedroom. "So I hear." He opened the front door, and he and Hollis stepped out onto the porch. It was cold, but there was something in the air–a breath of life, a whisper of hope. "Sap should run good today," he said.

Hollis took the steep steps two at a time, and ran to climb into his work clothes. There would be no school today for him, or any day in the next few weeks when the sap was running. "I wonder if Nicholas will know to come down?" he asked as he returned to the kitchen.

"Jock will know," Grandpa said.

Sure enough, when they arrived at the sugarhouse after breakfast and chores, Nicholas was waiting for them, talking to Gibby. After a quick round of greetings, they loaded the stacks of new buckets and the bags of spiles onto the sled. With Grandpa holding the reins, they headed into the sugarbush. Gibby carried a big drill that he called a "bit and brace". At each maple tree along the road he drilled one or more holes in the tree, a few feet up the trunk and all the way around it. The bigger the tree, the more holes he drilled. Into each of these holes Nicholas placed a spile, tapping it firmly in place with the back of a hatchet he carried. Sometimes the bark was so thick that he would have to use the hatchet to slice away a bit of the bark so the spile would reach the wood where the sweet sap flowed. Behind Nicholas walked Hollis, carrying pails and lids. Each bucket had a hole in its upper edge, which he hung from a small hook that stuck out of the underside of the spile. Hollis placed a lid on top of each bucket. It seemed like a lot of extra work, but Grandpa said it was worth the effort to keep rain, snow, bark and dirt out of the syrup. The job seemed endless as they worked up and down the many roadways.

When they had hung all of the buckets, they went back to the sugarhouse. First they set up the storage tank beside the back wall of the sugarhouse. Then they wrestled the large gathering vat, which had been stored behind the woodshed, onto the stone-boat and added a stack of gathering pails, buckets that had wire handles on them. Gibby and the boys donned yokes with pails and followed Grandpa and the team back into the sugar bush. Grandpa stopped the team at intervals and the younger men spread out, going from tree to tree with their gathering buckets. At each tree they removed the lid from the sap buckets hanging there and emptied each bucket into the gathering pails, and then replaced the bucket and lid on the tree. "Some of the sap buckets have hardly any in 'em," Hollis said. "Do you think we are gathering too soon?"

Grandpa gave his idea some consideration. "Nope," he said. "If we waited, by the time we get the back roads picked up, these buckets could be overflowing. We need to gather it fast and boil it fresh. You'll see how fast the vat will fill up."

When the gathering pails were almost too full to carry, they snowshoed back to the sled and emptied their buckets into the vat. Slowly, steadily they worked their way through the sugar bush, up one trail and down another, until Grandpa said it was time to take the vat back to the sugarhouse and empty it into the storage tank behind the sugarhouse. The boys unloaded the extra gathering pails and he turned the team. Gibby followed him down to the sugarhouse so he could bring the gathering vat back into the sugar bush, since Grandpa would stay and start the boiling.

While they were gone, Nicholas and Hollis continued their collecting. The snowshoes had begun to feel as if they were made of lead, and there was little wind left in their lungs for calling back and forth to each other, but occasionally they met at the road when they returned to exchange their full gathering pails for empty ones. "How much do you think we've got so far?" Hollis asked on one such meeting.

Nicholas shook his head. "I guess we've made a million trips each, with two three-gallon pails on each trip, so, what does that make it? About twelve million gallons?"

Hollis laughed. "Well," he said, "we'll 'gather it fast and boil it fresh!'"

"'Gather it fast and boil it fresh,'" Nicholas echoed, as he started back into the woods. That became their watchword, every time they met. "Gather it fast!" one would say. "Boil it fresh," the other would respond. It took their minds off their aching legs and shoulders.

After awhile they heard Gibby urging the team up the hill with the heavy wooden vat on the sled. He complimented the boys on the number of buckets they had filled and lined up beside the road while he was gone. As soon as those buckets were poured into the vat, they moved on.

The rest of the morning continued the same way, and at noon the boys followed the sled back down the hill. Long before the sugarhouse came into sight, they could smell the magical scent of wood smoke mingled with the maple steam. When they arrived at the sugarhouse, clouds of smoke and steam were billowing out of the open cupola on the roof, and inside, the sweet-smelling steam made it almost impossible to see Grandpa. Once their eyes grew accustomed to the indoor lighting they gathered around the evaporating pans to see how they worked. Grandpa showed them how the fresh watery sap flowed through a pipe from the storage vat outside and into the back pan, and then moved to the front pan as it thickened and became sweeter. He worked back and forth between the two bubbling pans, skimming foam from the surface and dropping it into a bucket. Then he tested the syrup to see if it was done. He dipped a large spoon into the pan and filled it. Raising the spoon over the pan, he tipped it and watched carefully as the syrup flowed off it back into the pan. "Is it ready?" Hollis asked eagerly.

"Not quite," Grandpa said. "See how it trickled off the spoon in a thin stream? That means we have to let it boil a little longer."

They watched a while longer, and Grandpa lifted out another spoonful. This time as he poured from the spoon, it spread out in a wide band. "Now it's ready!" Grandpa said. "See how it aprons off the spoon? That means it's done."

The boys watched intently as he prepared to draw off some of the finished syrup. The front tank had a spigot on it, and under that he placed a bucket that had layers of clean white flannel clipped over the top. He was just getting ready to open the spigot, when he stopped.

"Pour it, Grandpa," Hollis urged him.

"I almost forgot," Grandpa said. "I'm still not used to this new equipment. Before I draw off syrup, I have to make sure that fresh sap is flowing into the back pan. If I don't, the pan could go dry and burn the syrup. And if I let it go too long, it could cause a fire in the sugarhouse." He turned the spigot that allowed fresh sap from the storage tank to trickle into the evaporator pan, and then returned to the task of drawing off the syrup in the front pan. They all watched with delight as the thick golden liquid trickled down onto the flannel and filtered through it into the pail. Grandpa then filtered it again as he poured it into the barrel, or "settling tank," as he called it.

Hollis, eager to see the syrup put up in the cans, wanted to know why syrup that had been strained still had to go into the settling tank.

"You've got to let the 'sugar sand' settle out," Grandpa said. "Then it can be canned. Be patient. Time was," he said, gesturing at the little stove, "we would have been drawing off syrup earlier and finishing it in pots on the stove. With the new pans, it all gets finished without the extra work."

He opened the door of the arch and surveyed the fire. "How about you boys bring in a few armfuls of wood so I can stoke the fire? I've made so many trips to that wood shed, my leg feels like it could drop off!"

When the wood was brought in, Grandpa handed Hollis a fruit jar full of cold, clear liquid. "Take this to your grandma when you go over for dinner. She was feeling kind of poorly this morning, and fresh sap is a good tonic."

As Gibby, Hollis and Nicholas approached the house they could hear the sound of coughing. Upon entering, they found Grandma seated by the stove. The room was uncomfortably hot, but Grandma had a shawl pulled tightly around her shoulders, and was hunched up as though she was cold. Hollis realized with a start that he had never seen Grandma sitting down in the middle of the day, except for mealtime. When she saw them come in, she made an effort to get up, but she swayed on her feet for a moment and then dropped back into her chair.

Gibby took charge. "Hazel, you let me help you into your bed. You shouldn't be up."

Grandma protested, "I'll be all right in a minute. I just tried to get up too fast, that's all."

Gibby was firm. "Influenza is going around. The doc was out to our house yesterday for my ma. She looks just the way you do. Doc says get into bed and cover up."

Hollis remembered the jar of sap. "Here, Grandma," he said, offering her the jar. "Grandpa sent you some tonic to make you feel better."

Grandma reached out as if to take it, then said, "Later. I'll have it later," and collapsed onto her bed.

Hollis found the dinner she had prepared still on the stove, so they hurriedly ate, cleaned up their dishes, stoked the fire and packed a dinner pail for Grandpa. Hollis peered into Grandma's room. She seemed to be sleeping, so he tiptoed out, leaving the door ajar to allow heat to reach her.

The afternoon proceeded much like the morning, and Hollis, Nicholas and Gibby all returned to the sugarhouse with the last vat of sap just before dusk. They found Grandpa getting ready to shut down the evaporator. "I should boil some more tonight," he said, "but I'm worried about leaving Hazel alone, sick as she is. I've got to get back."

"Sanford, you go on home," Gibby said. "If you can spare me Hollis, we'll finish the boiling and clean up. We'll see you in the morning."

Grandpa hesitated a moment, then agreed. "I can do the barn chores alone. Keep the boy, and thank you." Worry lines creased his forehead. "We'll see what tomorrow brings." With that, he headed back to the house with Gwen and Jackie.

After making sure he was not needed, Nicholas left for his home, hurrying so he would make it before darkness fell. Gibby and Hollis stoked the fire and soon the sap was bubbling vigorously, and sweet, sticky steam engulfed them. Hollis returned to the woodshed for another load. "I wish they'd built the shed closer to the sugarhouse," he complained as he brought in the wood.

"It's safer, this way," Gibby said. "There's always a danger of a fire getting started in a sugarhouse, and having the woodshed attached makes the danger greater."

"If there's a chance the sugarhouse could catch fire, shouldn't we have some buckets of water nearby?" Hollis asked.

"That's a good idea, but haven't you hauled enough buckets for one day?" Gibby asked.

"A few more won't hurt, and besides, we'll need water for cleaning up." And so Hollis began what was to become his afternoon ritual of stocking the sugarhouse with buckets of clean water.

It took them about three hours to finish the boiling and wash all the equipment. Just when Hollis thought they were done and could finally go home, Gibby said, "Bring that little pan and a lantern and follow me." He picked up a large pot of boiling water on the stove and carried it out behind the sugarhouse to the storage tank. He splashed the scalding hot water over the sides and bottom of the tank. Next he did the same to the gathering tub. "Your grandpa wouldn't thank me to start him out in the morning with a sour tank and tub!" he said.

They closed up the sugarhouse for the night, each taking a lantern. The spring-like temperatures had dropped dramatically, and they buttoned their coats up to their chins. "Good," said Gibby. "It's turning cold."

"Won't that make the sap stop running?" Hollis asked worriedly.

"Just the opposite. You need the cold nights *and* warm days for sugaring. Otherwise the sap won't run. You've got to have both." Gibby headed out to the farm lane to go home, and Hollis, on snowshoes, took the shortcut around the pond. He could scarcely think of anything except how good his bed would feel when he reached it. Grandpa had left a lamp burning, and a plate of supper was in the warming oven above the stove. He realized with surprise that he was hungry, something he hadn't noticed in the drive to get the work done. He took the plate over to the table and sat down. Somewhere between the bacon and the fried potatoes, sleep overwhelmed him.

Grandpa found him at the table, his head propped on his hand, when he came out to get some cold compresses for Grandma. He smiled when he saw Hollis, understanding the bone-weariness that had overcome him. He shook Hollis by the shoulder. "Go up to bed, son," he said gently. "Tomorrow's another long day."

Hollis jerked awake, confused to find himself at the table. His bleary eyes took in the scene for a moment before he could get his bearings. "Grandpa," he said, "how's Grandma?"

Grandpa's face was grave. "She's got a terrible fever and I'm trying to bring it down with cold compresses. If she doesn't feel better by tomorrow, I'll have to go for the doctor. But that's tomorrow. Tonight you need your rest."

Hollis dragged himself up the steep stairs, the muscles in his legs crying out with each step. He barely remembered feeling his head hit his down-filled pillow.

He was awakened by murmuring voices downstairs in the kitchen. One was Grandpa, he knew, but the other voice was unfamiliar. His body ached for more sleep, but he pulled on his trousers to go downstairs and investigate.

Star Centerbar was warming herself beside the stove when Hollis emerged from the stairway door. She looked up. "Nicholas told me how ill your grandmother is. I came to help." She turned to Grandpa, continuing her earlier conversation. "When I was walking down the hill, I met up with the doctor. He was on his way to see Mrs. Lillibridge, and he had four other calls to make, all influenza, he thinks. He said he would come here when he is done. It is a terrible sickness, this influenza."

"I've given her some tea and put cold compresses on her," Grandpa said. "Her throat hurts, and she has a bad cough. And that fever just won't break. I don't know what else to do," he said, looking strangely frightened and helpless.

"You take a rest," Star said firmly. "I will sit with her awhile, and I have brought some special teas that will help." She took off her wraps and began bustling around the stove. Grandpa sank gratefully into his chair, too tired to argue.

"Hollis, you go back to bed, too," she said, and he was only too happy to obey. The next morning he awoke to the smell of bacon and coffee. The sky was growing light, and again he heard the rat-a-tat of melting snow. His legs ached when he swung them over the side of the bed. His arm ached when he poured water from the basin into the bowl. His shoulders ached when he pulled on his shirt. How would he ever get through another day of sugaring? He squared his shoulders. He just would, that's all.

Grandpa had already done the barn chores and was in seeing to Grandma when Hollis got downstairs. Star fixed him a plate, and watched with pleasure while he ate. "My Nicholas was so tired when he came home last night!" she laughed. "You, too?"

Hollis, his mouth full, nodded.

"And today, you will work again, too?"

Hollis nodded again. "The weather looks right," he finally managed.

"Nicholas will come again," she said. "I have put your dinner in a basket to take with you. It will save you time."

Seeing Grandpa come out of the bedroom, Hollis asked, "How's Grandma?"

"She seems to be resting a little better now," he said. "The doctor was here in the middle of the night. He said Star's teas were as good as any medicine he could prescribe, and that we just need to watch her and wait it out. It could take some time."

Star beamed at the praise. "You go on now. You go make your sugar," she said, making a shooing motion with her hands. "If there is any trouble, I can shout loud enough to call you back. Go on." She reinforced her instructions by putting the picnic basket into Grandpa's hands, and waved away his thanks.

Hollis picked up the lantern he had brought home the night before, and his snowshoes. Today Grandpa let him ride on the stone-boat with him. It was a precarious perch, and he almost fell off several times, but he was grateful for the ride. The sun was glistening off the snow, and the creek, swollen with melted snow, bubbled energetically toward the pond. Hollis could see a large dark spot in the middle of the snow-covered pond, where the invading creek was melting the ice. Across the meadow crows called back and forth.

Grandpa and Hollis arrived at the sugarhouse just behind Nicholas and Gibby.

"How's the missus?" Gibby wanted to know.

"She had a bad night, but Star came, and the doctor, too, and she's sleeping now," Grandpa said. "And your ma?"

"She's a bit better, thank goodness," Gibby said, "but it's a bad one that's going around. Some folks go into pneumonia. I hear they're shutting down the school till it's run its course. A lot of the older boys are off sugaring anyhow."

Grandpa grunted. "Well, speaking of sugaring, let's get at it. Those pails won't empty themselves!"

And so began another arduous day of tramping through the woods on snowshoes, hauling and pouring, hauling and pouring. Hollis and Nicholas ate their lunch in the sugar bush to save a trip down to the sugarhouse. The sap was flowing faster than it had the day before, and there was no time for rest. Their reward at the end of the second long day was the sight of a long row of freshly filled gallon syrup cans lined up on the sugarhouse shelf. A new chill in the air greeted them as they finished cleaning up the evaporator and scalding the gathering and storage tanks. Grandpa eyed the sky and noted the direction of the wind. "Clouds are coming in," he said.

"Is that bad?" asked Hollis.

"Not necessarily," Grandpa said. "Could be we'll get a good sugar snow tonight, the kind that sticks to the branches and trunks of the trees and makes the sap flow faster than ever. If we get more flow, we'd better be ready to boil 'round the clock. But if it stays frozen tomorrow, we get a day off."

While Grandpa drove the team home, Nicholas accompanied Hollis back to the house on snowshoes so he could walk home with his mother. When they entered the farmhouse they again heard the sound of coughing, but this time it was Star. Her eyes were glassy, and she had a blanket wrapped around her shoulders. Grandpa took one look at her and announced that he would be hitching the team up to the bobsled and driving Star and Nicholas home. Star protested, but she was too weak to argue for long.

Hollis looked in on Grandma and then dragged himself out to the barn to do the chores. It took a lot longer without Grandpa, but somehow he got through it, and Jessie forgave his amateurish attempts at milking and generously filled her pail. The house seemed strangely empty when he got back with the eggs and milk, and he busied himself to take his mind off it. He pumped water to fill the teapot, the wash pitchers and stove reservoir. Then he stoked the stove and split armfuls of kindling to refill the wood box. Finally he cleaned the glass chimneys on the kerosene lamps and lanterns, trimmed the wicks and lit them so the house would be bright when Grandpa returned.

That night they ate fried eggs and buttered bread that Grandpa toasted on the hot surface of the stovetop. Throughout the night Hollis was awakened several times by his grandmother's coughing. As it turned out, the next day was too cold for sugaring. When Hollis woke up the house was cold, so he went down to stoke the fire. It was unusual for Grandpa to sleep so late, but Hollis guessed that he was worn out from tending to Grandma during the night. He slipped on his coat and went outside. He groaned when he saw what the winds of the previous night had brought–fresh snow! With a sigh, he lifted the shovel off the nail on the porch and opened a path to the barn. The thought of all the sugaring roads that would need to be broken down again discouraged him. Why did it have to snow! And yet, Grandpa had said it might improve the flow....

The day of rest gave Hollis and Grandpa a chance to regain their energy and care for Grandma. Her fever was down some, but she couldn't shake the cough.

The doctor arrived around noon and said he was concerned by her cough and the sound of her chest. He feared pneumonia, and said she should not be left alone. "I know this comes at a bad time for you, Sanford, what with sugaring and all. I don't know anyone who can help out, though. Everyone's got sickness at their house."

Grandpa nodded. "It can't be helped. We'll do what needs to be done."

Hollis' heart sank. With Grandma so sick, there was no way that they could finish sugaring.

Grandpa seemed to read his mind. "I hate to leave you in the lurch, but you boys and Gibby can manage alone," he said. "You're a pretty good hand with Gwen and Jackie, so you and Nicholas can do the gathering while Gibby boils."

"We'll never be able to get to all the buckets before they overflow or sour," Hollis exclaimed, "not with me having to take the gathering tub back and forth!"

Grandpa thought for a minute, and then suggested, "Well what if you forget about those two back sections? Just leave them be, and concentrate on the lower ones. The runs to the sugarhouse will be shorter that way, and the sap will be fresh. It's better to do less and do it right."

Hollis agreed that that would work, and the next day, which was warmer, he set out across the meadow on the stone-boat behind Gwen and Jackie. Gibby had again brought the oxen, so once again they began the laborious job of breaking in the roadways so the horses could manage the sled with the heavy gathering tub.

They were nearly through when Nicholas showed up, breathless. "Sorry I'm late," he said, panting. "I ran most of the way. I had to help take care of my ma and fix breakfast for the little ones before I came."

Hollis explained the new plan that Grandpa had proposed, and they set to work collecting sap from the lower sections. As Hollis had predicted, it did go much slower, partly because of his inexperience with the team, but somehow they got through it. At the end of the day the row of filled syrup cans had grown.

When Hollis finished putting up the team, wiping them down and feeding them, he walked wearily back to the house. He paused to wash up at the pump and then went into the house.

A woman standing by the stove whirled to greet him. "Hollis!" Ma said.

"Ma! What are you doing here? How did you get here?"

"Frank Pasco stopped by the hotel this morning and said your grandma had the influenza and most of the neighbors were down with it, too. I just knew I had to come be here and help out. There's hardly any business at the hotel because of the sickness, so, when Frank offered to give me a lift, Mrs. Emerson told me to go along."

She gave him a big hug. "Your grandpa says you've been doing a man's work here," she said. "We're proud of you!"

"How did it go today?" Grandpa asked.

"Not too bad," Hollis said. "We did it the way you suggested and it worked all right."

"Well, thanks to your mother, tomorrow I'll be 'back in the traces,' as they say."

"How's Grandma?" Hollis asked.

"I'll let your Ma answer that," he said, "she's been doctoring away."

"I put a mustard plaster on her chest," Ma said, "and she seems to be breathing easier. It'll be a while before we can tell if she's on the mend. She'll have to be watched closely."

"How long can you stay?" Hollis asked.

"As long as I'm needed," Ma replied.

16

The Dream

It took Grandma all of sugaring season to regain her strength, and Mary stayed on to help. Hollis loved coming in each afternoon and seeing Ma at the stove or sitting with Grandma. The house sparkled again, the way it did when Grandma was well, and meals appeared on the table on schedule. On the days when it was too cold for sap to flow, Hollis was packed off to school to try to make up some of the work he had missed. On sugaring days, when Grandma was resting comfortably, Ma often hiked over to the sugarhouse to help Grandpa, filling cans, bringing in firewood or helping wash up. Despite the hard work and long hours, she looked happier than Hollis could ever recall seeing her.

During the fourth week of sugaring, the sap flowed so fast that they could hardly keep up with it. The sugarhouse shelves groaned under the weight of all of the filled syrup cans. It was dark on Tuesday when they brought the last vat of sap down, and the storage tank could barely hold it all. There were hours of boiling ahead, and it was already dusk.

Hollis made trips down to the pond and brought back pails of water to have on hand. "Grandpa, how long are you going to boil?" he asked.

Grandpa did some figuring. "My guess is, it'll take another four or five hours," he said, "if not more."

"Can I stay and learn how to run the evaporator?" Hollis asked.

Grandpa hesitated. "I guess I could use the help," he admitted, "but you'd have to go home and tend to the stock first."

Gibby and Nicholas chimed in, offering to help as well, but left for home when Grandpa said he was sure the two of them could handle it alone. Hollis set out across the pond meadow for the Ingraham house. Just as he came into the yard, he met Ma, coming out of the house with a picnic basket. "I figured you'd be boiling late, so I was going to take over some supper for you two," she said.

"I'm starving," Hollis said, "but I've got to go do the barn chores and bring feed back on the toboggan for the horses."

"I'll help you and it will go twice as fast," Ma said. When they got to the barn, Ma immediately settled down on the three-legged milking stool and began rhythmically filling Jessie's pail.

"Ma, you know how to milk?" Hollis asked in astonishment.

Ma laughed at his amazement. "When we lived on the farm I always did the milking. It was my favorite chore—so quiet and peaceful. I've missed it."

They breezed through the rest of the tasks and soon Hollis was on his way back to Grandpa with the basket and some hay and grain on the toboggan. He fed and watered the horses and then took the picnic basket to the sugarhouse. When he opened the door steam billowed out. He laughed when he got a good look at Grandpa, for his eyebrows were crusted with sugar deposited by the steam. Grandpa smiled with pleasure to see the picnic basket, and his grin broadened when he saw a small jar of fresh cream nestled in the tea towel that lined the basket.

"What's that for?" Hollis asked, since there didn't seem to be any coffee to pour it into.

"Your Ma remembered an old trick we used to use," Grandpa said. "Sometimes the sap boils way up, until it looks like it might go over the top of the pan. But if you drop a tiny speck of cream on top of it, it settles right down. Works every time. I'd almost forgotten."

While they ate, Grandpa talked about the evaporator, and how it worked.

"You see," he said, opening the door to feed the fire, "the arch is designed to pull the heat of the fire down through the box under the pans and over to the stovepipe." Hollis watched as he arranged some new pieces of firewood in the arch, being careful to allow air to move through the fire. The new wood burst into flames as it came into contact with the glowing hot coals. The bright orange flames licked the bottoms of the pans as they chased each other wildly to the stovepipe. The heat was intense. Grandpa shut the door and adjusted the airflow through the draft. "The pans are shallow and wide," he said, "so as the sap boils, the extra water in it boils off fast, leaving behind the thick, sweet syrup. Trouble is, you've got to watch it every minute. You don't want it to cook too long, or it gets dark." He opened the valve from the storage tank to let more sap into the back pan. "And you've always got to keep some sap in all the pans, or first thing you know you've got burning sugar in a pan, or, worse yet, the solder that holds the pan together melts and you've got your whole sugarhouse on fire."

Hollis listened closely. As the evening wore on, he and Grandpa settled into a sort of rhythm in the steamy sugarhouse. He brought in the wood, Grandpa stoked the fire and adjusted the draft. Grandpa adjusted the flow from the storage tank and between the pans, while Hollis skimmed and discarded the foam. Grandpa drew off a bucket of syrup and Hollis filtered it into the settling barrel. Grandpa filled some cans and Hollis checked the level of the storage tank.

During the occasional lull in their activity, they talked. Hollis found himself telling Grandpa the story Nicholas had told him about his last name, and the legend of St. Hubert. Grandpa listened thoughtfully until the tale was done. "So, you say the name isn't 'Centerbar,' like we all say?" he asked.

Hollis shook his head. "No," he said, "Nicholas called it 'Sant Eeyew-bare,'" he said, doing his best to reproduce the French syllables that Nicholas had pronounced.

"Hmmm," said Grandpa, "Seems like people oughta call them by their right name."

"I guess so," Hollis agreed, "but Nicholas said it didn't make much difference. He says that, as long as you know who you are and act the best you can, what people call you doesn't matter."

"That's true enough," Grandpa said, "but still, it doesn't seem respectful."

Their conversation was interrupted then, as syrup bubbled high in the pan, threatening to overflow. Grandpa's practiced hand flicked a speck of cream on it and the surge subsided. Then it was back to the routine of fetching wood, stoking, skimming, drawing off and straining. Over and over they followed this routine until Hollis could barely put one foot in front of the other. Grandpa, too, was moving more slowly, and seemed to be favoring his bad leg more than usual.

"You stretch out on that cot over there and catch forty winks," Grandpa said finally. Things have slowed down a bit, and I can watch it by myself for a while."

"Are you sure you don't need help?" Hollis made himself ask.

"I'm fine for now. I'll just sit here in the chair and take a little rest, too. I'll wake you in a while."

Too tired to argue further, Hollis sank gratefully onto the cot. Sleep flooded his senses. He lay dreamless and motionless, soaking up the rest that his body had ached for. Perhaps an hour passed before the faint stirrings of a dream intruded upon his sleep. Hollis dreamed he was in his bed at the farmhouse and Grandpa was banging the broomstick on the ceiling under his bed, telling him it was time to get up and do chores. He couldn't move. He was too tired. He scrunched down to sleep some more. The broomstick-rapping was replaced by an insistent voice, calling his name. "Hollis," the voice called. Hollis slept on. "Hollis!" the dream voice said more insistently, "Wake up, son!" In his dream he opened his eyes. Standing above him was the young man in the photo, the man with the square jaw and the laughing eyes. "Hollis, get up!" said the man, his father.

"Pa!" Hollis exclaimed, sitting upright on the tiny sugarhouse cot. The dream evaporated. His father was gone, and the sugarhouse was filled with steam. No, not steam, he realized immediately—smoke! He opened his mouth to cry out to Grandpa, but was caught up in a fit of coughing. The smoke choked his lungs and attacked his eyes. Above the evaporator arch he could see flames leaping toward the roof like dancing demons. "Grandpa, fire!" he managed through his coughing.

There was no answer. Where was Grandpa? Panic swelled in his chest as he struggled in vain to see his grandfather. Nearly overcome by the heat and smoke, Hollis sank to his knees. The smoke and heat were less intense there, and he was finally able to make out the form of his grandfather through the burning haze. He was still sitting in his rocking chair, and Hollis began crawling toward him, croaking as he went, "Grandpa! Grandpa!" He was within a few feet of the rocker when a river of fire flowed out of the sap pan and across the floor in front of him. Feasting on the pine floorboards, the flames began to grow and shoot upward. Hollis tried to leap across them, but was forced back as they lapped at his trouser legs.

Water! Where had he left the buckets of water? His eyes, bleary with tears from the smoky air, couldn't see them. He stooped down again and peered toward the door. He could just make out the cluster of buckets he had brought in at dusk. He crawled to the door, grabbed two of them, lurched to his feet and raced with them toward Grandpa's rocking chair. The heat was unbearable, but he had to get to Grandpa! He splashed water from one of his buckets on the burning floorboards, dousing those flames, at least for the moment. Fire still shot out of the top of the evaporator, where one pan had buckled grotesquely. He grabbed Grandpa's shoulder and shook him, but was unable to wake him. Was he alive? "Grandpa, please! Wake up!" he begged, gasping for breath.

Grandpa's chin was resting on his chest, and he could not be roused. Hollis grabbed the back of the rocker and prepared to drag it through the smoke-filled room. His lungs screamed for air. He could not last much longer. To his dismay, flames flickered again on the floorboards beside the chair. He dumped the other bucketful of water over them and summoned all his strength to lug the chair with Grandpa in it. It seemed like hours as he hauled the chair over the uneven boards to the door. A blast of delicious cold night air greeted them as the boy frantically hurled open the door and tried to wrestle Grandpa and the chair through it.

In the midst of the struggle, Grandpa began to cough. "Grandpa, we've got to get out of here," Hollis cried out. Grandpa nodded, indicating that he understood, and made an effort to stand. Hollis wedged his shoulder under Grandpa's arm, pushed the chair through the doorway and helped him outside. The flames, fed by the gust of air, roared with excitement. Hollis slammed the door. He was trembling as he and Grandpa stood together in front of the sugarhouse, coughing and wiping their eyes. It was a moment before they were able to speak.

"Are you all right?" Grandpa asked between coughs. "Are you hurt?"

"No, I'm all right," Hollis fibbed, not wanting to tell Grandpa yet about the blistering burns on his lower legs.

"I never could have forgiven myself if you'd been hurt. It's all my fault!" Grandpa said hoarsely. "I was supposed to be watching the pans and I fell asleep. Now everything will be lost," he said, looking at the flames inside. "All the syrup, all your hard work, the sugarhouse, all lost!"

"No, Grandpa, look!" Hollis said. "The fire didn't spread that far. It's all in the arch now."

Grandpa peered through the windows and realized that Hollis was right. The flames were all shooting up from within the stone firebox. "If those flames don't catch the rafters on fire, the rest of the sugarhouse should be safe!" he said.

Hollis wanted to carry more buckets of water inside the sugarhouse and douse the remaining flames, but Grandpa wouldn't let him. "The smoke is still heavy, and it's too dangerous to go in," he said. "Besides, letting in the air might make it worse. I think the rafters will be safe. We'll watch from here and let it die down naturally. If it doesn't," he began, then paused. "Well, if it doesn't, at least you're safe, and that's all that counts."

Hollis righted the rocking chair and set it on the ground in front of the sugarhouse so Grandpa could rest, and then got a log from the woodshed for himself to sit on. Together they kept a vigil, watching the flames settle down as the wood in the arch turned to coals. It was there that Ma found them when she came across the pond meadow with a lantern.

"Why, what are you two doing out here?" she asked merrily. "I thought you'd still be boiling. I came to—" She stopped abruptly when she saw their soot-streaked faces lit by the flickering flames from the sugarhouse. "What happened?" she exclaimed.

It was Grandpa who answered. "I told the boy to take a nap while I watched the pans," he said. "I fell asleep, and the pans caught fire. If the boy hadn't woken up...." He didn't finish the sentence. They all knew what would have happened if they had continued to sleep. Ma shuddered.

A few minutes later Grandpa declared it safe to go inside, and they surveyed the damage. The pans were ruined. Their seams had melted, and the pans had twisted all out of shape. On the far side of the arch, Grandpa spotted the charred floorboards, still wet and smoldering. His eyebrows shot up. "I was sitting right here! Right next to where these boards are burned! Did you soak this down?"

Hollis nodded. "I used some of the wash water."

"I would've been a goner. All I can remember is coughing and choking, and then you were helping me out the door."

Ma's voice trembled as she said, "It's a miracle you woke up in time, Hollis!"

For the first time Hollis thought of the strange dream that had awakened him. He remembered the laughing eyes and the gentle, insistent call. "Yes," he said softly, "a miracle." Perhaps some day he would tell Ma about his dream. Grandpa doused the embers in the arch, and the three Ingrahams latched the sugarhouse door, collected the team and went home.

Hollis and Grandpa returned to the sugarhouse early the next morning, and Gibby and Nicholas, unaware of the events of the previous night, showed up on schedule, planning to gather sap as usual. They were astounded to hear about the fire and of Hollis' and Grandpa's miraculous escape. They exclaimed over and over again about how fortunate it was that Hollis had awakened and had been able to get Grandpa out. They had to inspect the bandages Ma had put on Hollis' legs.

Grandpa led the way into the sugarhouse, where they looked over the mess created by the fire. It was obvious that, even if the pans could be repaired, the time required to fix them would waste most of the rest of the season.

"Or," Gibby suggested, "we could finish out this year with the iron kettles."

"I don't think so," said Grandpa. "We've had a good run, and we have a lot of gallons to go to market. What with the warm weather, the sap has begun to get that 'buddy' taste. I don't like to sell the late season syrup."

"So you want to wrap it up for this year?" Gibby asked.

"What do you think, partner?" Grandpa asked Hollis.

Hollis hesitated. He was flattered that Grandpa would ask his opinion. Part of him wanted to keep going and make as much syrup as they could. But, after thinking for a moment, he said, "Didn't Pa buy the pans in order to get the best syrup possible? If we use the kettles now, and boil buddy sap, the evaporating pans were for nothing. I think we should stop now."

"You don't want to get all the money you can this year?" Grandpa pressed him.

"No," said Hollis firmly. "I want people to know that Ingraham and Ingraham make the best pure maple syrup around, even if it means having less to sell."

"Then it's settled," Grandpa said, looking pleased at his decision. "We'll clean up this mess, market the syrup we've made so far, and divide up the profits. Next year will be a new opportunity."

Then the work began. Gibby and the boys dragged the ruined pans outside. Grandpa lit a fire in the woodstove, and Hollis and Nicholas hauled water to be heated for cleaning up the equipment. More water was heated to scald the storage tank and gathering vat, and then Gibby and the boys began making trips to the woods to collect the buckets, lids and spiles. The warm weather had melted much of the snow, so they were able to trek to the trees without the cumbersome snowshoes. When they returned to the sugarhouse with the last of the equipment on the sled, Ma had joined the work party.

There was plenty of work for all. Pails and pails of water were heated to wash all of the buckets, lids and spiles. The boys took the clean equipment outside to dry, lining the spiles and lids up on boards and stacking the overturned buckets in large pyramids to dry in the sun.

When they closed up the sugarhouse at the end of the day there was just one more task to complete. Hollis and Ma and Grandpa returned the next morning to carefully paste on each can a large, white label that declared "Ingraham & Ingraham, Thurman, NY, Pure Maple Syrup." The syrup was ready for market. Mr. Pasco would take some, of course, but most of it would go to fill an order from a large store in Saratoga Springs. Grandpa would take it down on the train on Friday and return on Saturday.

Saturday! Hollis could hardly wait. Grandma, who was almost back to her old self, had announced that there was to be a jack wax party on Saturday. "It's too much for you, what with you just getting over the influenza," Grandpa had argued.

"Nonsense," Grandma, declared. "It'll be like old times, and it's just the medicine we've all needed! Besides," she said, smiling at Ma, "Mary's here to help."

With the help of Gibby and Nicholas, word circulated around Kenyontown that there would be a party at the Ingraham farm. By early Saturday afternoon a steady stream of neighbors flowed toward the farmhouse. They came mostly on foot, since the warm weather had melted much of the snow, leaving sticky mud in its place. Mud season was too late for a sleigh and too early for a wagon.

There were the Centerbars, the Websters, the Goodnows, the Pascos, Miss Kenyon, and so many others it was hard to believe they could all fit into the house. As it turned out, many spilled out onto the porch to visit in the mild weather. Some of the men walked to the barn to talk about stock and spring planting. Others went to the sugarhouse, asking to hear again the story of the fire and rescue. The children raced and played games outdoors.

The guests all came bearing food. There were pots of baked beans, kettles of stewed chicken, pork or beef, and pans of sausages, as well as cakes, salads, pies, loaves of bread, and jars of jam or pickles. Some of the contributions went into Grandma's big oven, while others were placed on the makeshift serving table that had been improvised from saw horses and boards on the porch. Grandma, Ma and Julia Goodnow took turns stirring the huge pan of maple syrup that had monopolized the top of the stove for the better part of the day.

Gibby arrived rolling a barrel in front of him. Hollis ran out to greet him. "What's in the barrel?" he wanted to know.

Gibby rolled it to the shady side of the house and stood it upright. "Take a look," he invited.

Hollis pried the lid off the barrel. He found it packed full of pure white snow. He looked at Gibby in amazement.

"It's for the jack wax. You'll see!" Gibby said, laughing.

Hollis had no longer to pursue the subject, for guests were beginning to load up their plates with the delicious food, and he couldn't resist getting into line for his own dinner. He and Nicholas sat on the edge of the porch with their plates on their laps and their legs dangling down, eating until they were stuffed. They had just taken their plates into the kitchen, when the crowd began clamoring for music. Grandpa took his fiddle down from the clock shelf and tuned it up. He began playing a merry reel, and no one could resist the lively beat. Some were tapping their toes and others clapped in time. Jock Centerbar pulled a harmonica from his pocket and began to play along. Ira Goodnow fished a couple of spoons out of the dishpan, dried them off on his shirttail, and, holding them in one hand, alternately rattled them together and slapped them against his leg to the beat of the music. Frank Pasco danced a little jig until the tune ended amid a round of applause.

The music didn't stop for long. Immediately someone called out for a waltz, and when the waltz ended, another cried out for a square dance. There was barely room to move, but somehow, amid much cheering and laughter, the dancers executed the spins, the dos-a-dos and the allemande lefts as Ira called them out. More and more tunes were requested, until finally Grandpa said they would play just one more song before taking a little rest. He turned to the gathered crowd. "Let's ask our neighbor, Jacques St. Hubert"—he took great care to pronounce it exactly as Hollis had pronounced it–"if he will play us one of his French Canadian tunes."

Jacques looked at Grandpa with surprise, but his pleasure at being addressed by his correct name was evident in his broad smile. He raised the harmonica to his lips, took a deep breath and began to play. The haunting strains of a waltz soon had the party guests swaying back and forth. Miss Kenyon and a young man from Athol took the floor, followed by Ma and Gibby. A few others joined in as Grandpa accompanied him on the fiddle. The song ended with more enthusiastic clapping and pleas for the musicians to resume playing soon.

The crowded little house had become uncomfortably warm and stuffy, so Nicholas and Hollis went out onto the porch. In a few minutes Grandpa and Grandma, and Gibby and Ma joined them.

"There you are!" Grandpa exclaimed. "We've been looking for you. It's time to talk a little business.

Hollis and Nicholas exchanged glances, wondering what was coming next.

Grandpa pulled from his pockets some envelopes. "The syrup has been sold, and now it's time to settle up. Gibby," he said, extending one envelope, "this is your share." He handed another to Nicholas. "And here's yours, Nicholas. You're a fine worker."

The last envelope was for Hollis. "Hollis," Grandpa said, "This is for you. I've put my share in with yours, because if you hadn't gotten this notion, we never would have tapped the trees this year. And if you hadn't woken up in time to put out the fire, there wouldn't have been any syrup to sell. And we might not be here today at all."

"Grandpa," Hollis protested, "that's not fair! Some of this has to be for you!"

"Son," Grandpa said, putting his hand on Hollis' shoulder, "the way I see it, it's all for me, because it's for the family. I know that you've been wanting to raise money to help your ma get squared away with her bills. I owe her a big debt, too. If she hadn't come and nursed your grandma through the influenza, where would we have been? And if she and your pa hadn't sacrificed to buy the pans, we wouldn't have had them to use. It's the least I can do, after the stubborn old fool I've been."

Grandma just beamed, saying nothing. Hollis handed the envelope to Ma.

Nicholas broke the silence. "Thank you for my share. My ma will be able to buy things that she needs at the store. It will be a big help to my family."

"Your ma and pa should be very proud of you," Grandpa said. "How about you, Gibby? Have you made plans for your share?"

Gibby shuffled from one foot to the other. Hollis had never before seen him at a loss for words, and was puzzled. "Well," Gibby managed finally, "I was thinking maybe if I put my share in with yours and the boy's, Sanford, we might just get this gal to leave Warrensburg and move out to Thurman."

Ma blushed at this, but couldn't help smiling. She looked into Hollis' envelope, and her eyes widened. "From the looks of this, there will be enough in here to finish settling up my accounts and replace the damaged evaporator pans! It looks like Ingraham and Ingraham will be back in business next year," she said.

Gibby had a quick response. "Well, then," he said, glancing shyly at Ma, "You know that sixty acres my Pa deeded over to me? My share could buy the rest of the lumber I need to start building a house on it." He paused, looking meaningfully at Ma, and then Hollis. "I'm sure I could build it big enough for three."

Ma blushed a deeper shade of red. She took Gibby's hand and said nothing, but her smile answered his unasked question. Hollis grinned from ear to ear. At that precise moment, Julia Goodnow called from the kitchen. "Gibby, better get that snow up on the porch now. The jack wax is ready!" Gibby sighed, reluctantly released Ma's hand and went to get the barrel of snow.

All the guests lined up with plates and bowls, and Gibby packed a generous pile of snow on each dish. One by one they filed up to the kitchen stove where Julia dipped her ladle into the thickened maple syrup and generously drizzled the golden nectar over their snow. Hollis took his plate back out onto the porch. He watched as the others savored their treat, and followed their example, poking his fork into the gooey jack wax and twirling it around to pick up a bite. He had never tasted anything so wonderful in his life. The rich maple treat melted in his mouth and trickled down his throat. It felt like heaven. "There's nothing like Ingraham syrup," he heard Ira Goodnow say.

Hollis' eyes were drawn to the late winter sun as it slipped behind Crane's gracious curves. Suddenly overwhelmed with all that had happened to him, Hollis slipped away from the crowd and walked toward the pond, along the old path now etched anew in the melting snow. He paused by the pond's edge to think. That autumn night in Warrensburg when Ma told him he was to move to Thurman seemed a lifetime ago. How much he had learned since then, and how much had changed. He could never have guessed back then that the trip that felt like the end of his life would in fact be a new and wonderful beginning.

The raspy sound of Grandpa's fiddle drew his attention back to the cozy house stuffed full of friends and family. The little farm-house began to fade into the dusk, and then sprang back to life as Ma and Grandma lit lamps and placed them in the windows. Gibby appeared on the porch and hung a lantern from the rafters. Hollis could hear the laughter and feel the love. Happiness washed over him, for he realized what true treasure was. He had found it.

A Lantern at Dusk